I0578597

THE GIRL HE LOVES

A SECOND CHANCE ROMANTIC COMEDY

KRISTI ROSE

Copyright © 2020 by Kristi Rose

All rights reserved.

No part of this book may be reproduced in any form or by any electronic or mechanical means, including information storage and retrieval systems, without written permission from the author, except for the use of brief quotations in a book review.

Publisher's Note: This is a work of fiction. Names, characters, places, and incidents are a product of the author's imagination. Locales and public names are sometimes used for atmospheric purposes. Any resemblance to actual people, living or dead, or to businesses, companies, events, institutions, or locales is completely coincidental.

Vintage Housewife Books

Cover Design © 2022 Qamber Designs and Media

The Girl He Loves/ Kristi Rose. -- *1st edition*

ISBN: 979-8-684430-16-9

CHAPTER 1
FRIDAY

Today's the day. Finally. Sure, getting here took me way longer than I initially planned. But I'm here. I sit before my counselor because today I'll be assigned my student teaching placement. This is the final step in finishing my Bachelor's Degree in elementary education. Only two classes remain that I'll complete over the summer, then student teaching in the fall, after which I don a cap and gown and fulfill the dream.

"We've run into a bit of a hiccup," says Rebecca Jamison, my college counselor, while not making eye contact.

I shift in my seat. "What do you mean a hiccup?"

This moment is huge for me. I'm finally going to finish college. I should have graduated from my first go at college eight years ago, but life, in my case an unexpected pregnancy, derailed me. And yes, I had hoped to finish two years ago when I made a second attempt. But who's counting? Only me and the X-marks I make on the calendar every day. I'm here now. I'm so close I can taste it. And it's yummy. That's why "hiccups" are unwanted.

Jamison, my steadfast administrative cheerleader, acts differently today. Today it seems our roles are reversed. I came into her office relaxed and confident of the next step. Yet she sits across from me worrying one hand by rubbing the tips of her fingers together. Her office, beige walls with worn beige carpet, is decorated with inspirational posters. Mountains calling people to go the distance. Einstein's profile telling us we are smart. Which is like a joke in comparison. But whatever.

Three and a half ago years ago when I sat in her office, in this same seat with the worn armrest, I'd been the worried one. A single mom with no extra cash to spare, I wasn't sure I could afford to go back to college. Jamison told me then there would no obstacle we couldn't overcome. She'd been right, mostly. I've had a few setbacks like having to take a semester off for my son's hospitalization, but that was unavoidable. Or having to lighten my load because my ex-husband wasn't co-parenting like a good father is supposed to. Never mind his habit of being consistently delinquent with child support.

Jamison taps a piece of paper with her other hand and sucks in a deep breath. As she exhales, she says in a rush of words, "Let me explain, Heather. You see, when people apply to the university to be a teacher, we do a background check. We do this because, in order to work in a school setting or with children, the applicant can't have a criminal record." She casts me a fleeting glance.

I nod in agreement. I don't have a criminal record, and what she says makes sense. Would I want someone with a criminal record working with my child? I suppose it would depend on the crime, but as with all humans, my mind leaps to the worst so my gut reaction is no. Nope. Nada.

That's why what Jamison says makes sense.

I wait for her to continue.

Her gaze stays on something over my shoulder, but I resist the urge to look behind me.

She says, "When you applied, we did that standard background check. Only there seems to have been a slight error."

I lean forward when she says error. "Go on."

"At the time you enrolled, an intern was doing the background checks. She goofed and marked yours as passed. Only there's no documentation to prove it."

"I submitted fingerprints," I say. "Do I need to do those again?"

Jamison holds up her hands as she continues to explain. "No, your fingerprints are fine."

I shake my head in confusion. "I don't understand."

She clears her throat. "Once we have fingerprints, we submit them to the FBI in what's called a level two screening. This screening looks for certain misdemeanors or felonies. The FBI will then complete the screening and respond with a printable document that shows a pass or fail. We can only assign student teaching placement to students who have a pass on that document. Your file didn't have that piece of paper, even though all your other essential documents were present. It's unfortunate this error wasn't caught when you started, but here we are." She says the last bit to herself. "We ran yours again and, um, yours came back with an issue." She drew out the words as if she was afraid to say them.

"An issue?" I repeat. "I don't have a criminal record so I can't imagine what issue there is. My ex-husband is delinquent with his child support payments, but why would that show up as an issue for me? I mean, it is financially. Did

Justin file a complaint about the threat I made if he didn't make those payments sooner rather than later? Nah, any moron listening to our conversation could surmise I'd made the threats out of anger. The day I no longer have to depend on his financial support will be amazing.

I continue, "Perhaps you should run them again because it sounds like an error on their end." It's possible the FBI goofed, right?

Jamison glances down at her desk and lifts the edge of a piece of paper. "Were you not arrested for indecent exposure, um, nine years ago?"

The memory hits me, that day coming back in a flash. I groan and roll my eyes. "Well, I was arrested—the cop was new and overzealous—but I wasn't charged. We were sunbathing on the roof of the sorority house."

"We" being half of my sorority. Thirteen of us were taken to the station, but charges were never filed. "The courts made us pay a citation. They said it was like getting a driving ticket. We paid a small fee. Well, not really small. It was a thousand dollars but once we paid, they sent us on our way with a slap on the wrist." And for our roof top fun we were rewarded with a sunburn on areas I hope never see the sun again.

Not that I ever told my parents about the slap on the wrist because I was mortified. I mean, who gets in trouble for nude sunbathing on a rooftop? We purposely went up on the rooftop so no one would see us, and yet somebody saw with binoculars from an apartment building a block away, or wherever, and called the police.

Jamison presses her lips together briefly before she says, "That may be, but according to this piece of paper" — she taps the sheet on her desk again — "you were arrested for indecent exposure, which is a misdemeanor in the first degree. The law in Florida states a charge in the first degree, and one that's an indecent exposure, will keep you from working with children."

This time she looks at me, pity in her eyes.

I bluster, "But—but I wasn't charged."

She gives me a sad smile. "In Florida, being arrested creates the record. Charged or not."

I groan and drop my head into my hands. "You have got to be kidding me! I'm so close to finishing. So close to turning my life around and making real money. Well, more than I make now in retail anyway. Now you're telling me I just spent over three and a half years and accrued butt loads of student loans working on a degree that I can't have?"

I study her from between my fingers.

She says, "Well, you can try to have your record expunged. But that takes time. You can't do your student teaching until this matter is all cleared up."

"And what if I can't get my record expunged?"

Jamison sighs. "You won't be able to teach." She holds up her hand. "But we can shift you to a different track."

I snort with derision. My degree track is elementary education. But my plan wasn't to stop there. "You said once I got this degree, I could then do online school and get my certification in special education. What am I supposed to do with these classes if I can't use them to teach special needs kids?"

"If you get the record expunged between now and September, I can get you on the list for a spring internship starting in January. That puts your graduation out by six months, assuming getting your record removed goes smoothly. Six months isn't so long."

I stand on the precipice of a full-blown pity party. Or at the very least a good old-fashioned crying fit. Six more months? That feels like forever. And that's if things go smoothly. My odds of winning the lottery are probably higher than getting something to run smoothly.

Yet, I've persevered. I've stayed strong. I kept swimming. However you want to phrase it, I've held fast to the belief that if I worked hard to improve my life, I'd succeed.

The last five years have been really crappy. I mean, I'm living proof of that saying: "the hits just keep on coming."

First, I discover my son has epilepsy. Ever experience your kid having a seizure? Moms out there whose kids have seizures know how scary that is. Like *suck the breath out of you* scary and leave you trembling for days. I'm not saying there aren't other scary things, but this is *my* scary thing and sits right at the top of my "things that scare the shit out of me" list.

Then my marriage fell apart. Secretly, I'm kind of okay about that. Would I like to have a partner who splits the chores, worry and expenses with me? Absolutely, but my ex-husband Justin wasn't a partner. He was the dude who brought home money and wanted sex. Sex that wasn't even that good.

We married for the wrong reasons, though our intentions were noble. But I don't miss him. I miss the child support money because I live paycheck to paycheck.

And now, here I am.

I say, "You know, Mrs. Jamison, all this information would have been helpful before I borrowed forty thousand in student loans to get this degree. And now you're telling me I can't even use it, much less graduate, unless I can get my record expunged?"

She pats down the air between us with her hands, as if to say "bring it down, relax, chill." None of which I'm capable of doing.

Mrs. Jamison says, "You can graduate on time. But to do so we'll need to shift you to a different track, a different degree in the same sort of field, because you can't do your student teaching. But there are lots of things you can do. You know, you can, uh…" She glances down at a piece of paper where she's clearly written out a list of these new and grand occupational opportunities.

"You could be a corporate trainer. You could be a college academic advisor."

I close my eyes. "Isn't that working with children? I mean, just because they're 18…."

"Well, they're legal adults, so…"

"Oh, so it's okay to have an indecent exposure record and work with so-called legal adults who can't even buy liquor, but that's fine. I get it."

I really didn't, but whatever.

When I started college the first time, it was to major in psychology, which I never finished, and here I am again, second time around, with a degree in a different field that I can't finish either. Kinda feels like this isn't meant to be.

Jamison continues, "You could be a sales rep. Oh, a real estate agent."

I hate to be a Debbie Downer, but that train has left the station. I say, "I could've done all that without getting a degree. I pursued this degree because I want to work with children like my son. I want to help other families. I want to help other kids. I want to give parents hope, to know they are more than the sum of their problems or their child's diagnosis. That maybe not all their hopes and dreams for their child are gone."

She smiles sadly. "You could be a tutor."

I shake my head in confusion. "I'm sorry. I could be a tutor? Isn't that working with children?"

"Yes, but if you do it privately, you don't have to disclose anything."

This was a joke, right? "Oh, okay. So, ethically, I can just put my morals aside. That's good to know." I make a mental note to have every person who ever privately worked with my child fingerprinted. I'm realistic enough to know not everyone in this world is upstanding.

Dear Lord, I'm a hypocrite.

Jamison keeps on with her list. "How about a museum curator?"

"How does my degree in special education transfer over to a museum curator?"

She shrugs helplessly. "I don't know, Heather. I looked over your transcripts. You have a fair amount of options. You almost finished your psychology degree, and you have a minor in art. You have a lot of credits. I'm sure we can find something. Either way, you need to decide. Do you want this degree, or do you want to graduate when you planned? Or are you willing to put everything off by a year max? Those are the options to get you to graduation."

I say, "Okay. I think I should talk to a lawyer before I make any decisions. I have a friend who might be able to help me out and expedite this. Is there any chance I get could on this internship rotation if she can turn this around rapid fast?"

Jamison grimaces. "Well, technically no."

I rear back, stunned. Man, the day was beginning to super suck. "Oh, I see. I guess that's it then."

She holds up a hand. "But I can give you until Tuesday of next week."

It's midday Friday, and I doubt I can find the right lawyer over the weekend. So, essentially that gives me Monday to find a lawyer and that person precious little time to see if my quest to clear my record is even possible.

"I'm sorry, Heather," she says. "Your grades are exceptional, so transferring to another program isn't going to be a problem. You'll be accepted into almost anything."

"Except the one thing I want to do," I say sadly.

CHAPTER 2

FRIDAY

I leave Jamison's office disheartened and frustrated. And, honestly, scared. I don't want to be the sort of person who gets caught up in a freak-out, stuck in a negative cycle, but I was seconds from needing to breathe into a brown paper bag to calm myself down.

I think of those movies where the person losing their mind gets slapped. I need a slap, only slapping myself wouldn't be effective. It wouldn't pack the right heat. Instead, I do what might be the equivalent of a slap. I call my mom.

Wrapping my mind around this is hard. I need to focus on the big picture. Like: if I change degree tracks, how much more time in school would be required, and how much more in student loans would I have to take out? I was focused solely on getting what I wanted. My teaching degree.

I wish I could be blasé about debt. I have plenty of it. School loans, medical debt, and the standard mortgage. But I'm treading water here, barely keeping myself afloat. Sitting in my minivan, which I also owe money on, I lean back against the seat and close my eyes while the phone rings, waiting for my mom to answer.

"Hello, sweetheart," my mom says. She does this sing-song voice when she's in a good mood. "How'd it go at school?"

I skim over the topic. "Fine. How are things there? How's Tyler?" Thankfully, she's a free and willing babysitter, which comes in handy on days Tyler's school is out, like today. And, when she watches Tyler at my house, she cleans. Win-win. Guess that's one silver lining today.

"Oh, it's all going beautifully." The swish-swish of a squirt bottle sounds through the phone.

"Really?" I say. My son, almost eight, can be a bit of a... pistol. And he knows Mimi loves to spoil him, so he really works her to get what he wants.

"He's out in the backyard playing flag football with Uncle Doug. He's burning energy and having a ball."

"Why's Doug there? Doesn't he have a job?" Not that I don't love my brother, but when he stops by uninvited, it's usually to deliver a talking down or a handout or something else demoralizing. "And why is Tyler playing flag football? You know I don't like him playing contact sports. I don't think it's a good idea. What if he has a seizure?"

"Oh, Heather, let him be a child. He could have one while watching TV, and you let him do that."

Easy for her to say. She's never seen him have a seizure. "He's sitting in a chair when he watches TV, not in motion like playing football. He's running down the backyard waiting to be tackled." I glance at the smartwatch I wear, provided to me as part of an epilepsy study Tyler and I are doing. The watch's purpose is to alert me when Tyler's having a seizure. I tap the face, but it stays green, the color that means everything's good, and the only thing displayed on the face is the time.

"Nobody tackles anyone in flag football. They just pull a flag off the strap on your waist and they're laughing and having fun. This is what children are supposed to do." She reminds me.

Yes, I agree. Children are supposed to laugh and be carefree. Children aren't supposed to have epilepsy. Children aren't supposed to have autism or cancer or anything else that hijacks their childhood. But children do. And then they have parents who just want to make sure they're safe and grow up healthy. But I don't say this to my mom because it's an old argument.

"Why did Doug come by?"

"Oh, your dishwasher was acting up, so I had him pop over to take a look."

I groan. "Mom, did you not see the note I left? The dishwasher's been acting up for a while. I hope you didn't run it?" I left a bolded large-print note taped to the dishwasher with the warning.

"I did, but don't worry, I mopped up after it flooded the kitchen."

I slap my palm against my head.

"I was going to mop anyway. At least it's done," she says.

See? Silver lining. My floor is now clean.

This time she switches the subject. "Tell me what the counselor said. Did you get a placement at Tyler's school?"

Funny how my biggest concern this morning was where I'd do my student teaching. I wanted it to be in Tyler's school, worried that if it wasn't I'd have to juggle both Tyler and our differing schedules. Naive, when will I ever learn?

"I'll know more Tuesday," I say to deflect. "There are

some things that need to be resolved on their end before more placements can be finalized."

"But you told them you wanted Tyler's school?"

"They know that."

"You should have reiterated it."

"Quick question. Who's that lawyer Dad plays golf with?" Because I want to make sure I don't call him when I seek services.

If I can get my record expunged, my parents need never know about this latest obstacle, and what caused it. I mean, I already got the lecture about dropping out of college. I already got the lecture on getting pregnant while in college, which is why I dropped out. Then I got the side-eyes and little retorts when Justin and I separated. Now that we're divorced, I don't dare tell my family he's consistently delinquent with child support because somehow they'd make that my fault, too. No need to add to the list. I'll come up with something believable if this can't be resolved quickly.

"His name is Robinson, Mitch Robinson. He's a criminal attorney. Heather, you don't need a criminal defense attorney, do you?"

I'm not surprised she makes that leap.

"No, Mom. I'm asking for a friend." Thank heavens, Mom isn't on Facebook and doesn't know the inside joke of "asking for a friend."

"Oh, dear. You have a friend in trouble. It's not one of the girls, is it? Because you know if I had to pick one, it would be that Josie."

"No, mom, it's not Josie—who, by the way, is a lawyer." I should've called her. But I know why I didn't. Because I hate that all my friends are successful and going places and I'm...

Right where I've always been. And I need yet another handout.

"Are you and Tyler still okay with me going to work at the fundraiser?" I ask. I volunteered to waitress at an epilepsy fundraiser today.

"Yep, we've got the day all planned out. You take some time for you. Celebrate. You're almost done with school, and your dad and I are so proud. Let today be a small gift from us."

I suck a deep breath in through my nose, yoga style. "Thanks Mom. Tell my kid I love him. I'll try to call around dinner."

We hang up after a few more words.

Before I drive away, I do an internet search for expunging records and lawyers who do this sort of thing in Daytona Beach. Ads for various firms pop up.

Get your record clean in two to six months. Prices start at $1000.

Okay. That's a start. I will offer Josie that amount. The cost sucks, but it gives me an idea of what dealing with this issue will entail. What the baseline cost will be. I mean, if I were going to blow a thousand dollars, would this be what I would spend it on? No. Maybe I would buy myself something or get a new dishwasher. And I'd take myself and my child out to eat, too. Haven't done that in a while.

Big picture, a grand is small to get what I want, right? Though with my luck, it'll probably cost something ridiculous, like six grand.

I click on one of the ads for the expunging company. Is that even the right word? Expunging? Sounds like there's mold or something on my roof, *expunge*.

My next call is to Josie. But after four rings, the call goes to voicemail. Josie is also working at the epilepsy fundraiser, so I know I'll see her there. Nothing more I can do now. I will myself to set the problem aside. Once I'm done working the fundraiser, I'll devote all my attention to this issue.

Though if I had one wish, it would be...what? Truth is, if I had one wish, it would be that my child wouldn't have epilepsy. But I pretend that wish has already been granted and I've been gifted another one today. Lucky me. And so, I'll wish for...a resolution that won't break the bank and will give me what I want.

A glance at the clock on my minivan's dash tells me I'm supposed to be back in Daytona Beach in an hour and a half for my assigned shift with the fundraiser. The drive from the campus to downtown Daytona is just shy of an hour.

Leaving the campus of the University of Central Florida, I point my minivan north, take 417 through Sanford and catch I-4 at Seminole. The scenery is so familiar I don't really see it. Palm trees, lakes, and strip malls. Fifty minutes later, I'm exiting onto International Speedway Boulevard, and I don't remember anything about the drive. I was on autopilot. I've done it three times a week for the last two years. I don't recall seeing any of the landmarks, signs for new Disney attractions, or even crossing lanes to get to the off-ramp, which is pretty scary when you think about it. No cell phone necessary to cause my distracted driving today.

At a red light, my phone pings. The text message from Mom is a picture. Tyler at the Kona Shaved Ice truck. He's holding a giant blue shaved ice, and his lips are already stained. His smile is infectious.

The caption from Mom is *This kid finds joy everywhere.*

I bang my head against the steering wheel twice and am going for a third when the car behind me honks.

Big picture, right? Who cares that my degree track just went sideways, my dishwasher is leaking, the roofer I hired after the last hurricane did a terrible job and I suspect that's leaking as well, and my ex hasn't paid child support in two months.

I'll get past this obstacle like I've done every other. Tyler is healthy and his seizures are currently managed, and as much as I hate that he's playing football, I know that he's loving it. What kind of mom would begrudge that? Not this kind. Even though I worry.

My mom's right. I'm going to enjoy tonight. I'm going to laugh with my friends who are also working the fundraiser, and I'll be raising money for a worthy case.

Anything else this day wants to throw at me, I'll simply swat it to the ground. Like the pesky issue it'll probably be. I'm more than this hurdle.

Bring it, universe! It's going to take more than topless sunbathing to bring me down!

CHAPTER 3
FRIDAY

BIKE WEEK OFFICIALLY STARTS TODAY. CLOSE TO HALF A MILLION people, a large majority on motorcycles, pour into Daytona Beach and surrounding towns and clog up the roads. This isn't their fault. To manage the congestion, the city is forced to rope off several roads, turning them into one-way streets as one of Daytona's biggest tourist events explodes onto the scene.

The sun is bright and warm, and women clad in bikinis ride behind men dressed in head to toe leather. Mufflers pop around me as people gun their bikes.

Between this and race week, the locals have become desensitized. Now the rev of a motorcycle is like white noise.

The Fox and Hound restaurant, known for its traditional English fare and pub atmosphere, was started by my friend Jayne's parents, and is kicking off the ffundraising event. Each night for the next week, a different local restaurant is slotted to "pop up" in the empty parking lot across from the beach and one block north of the most popular bar on the strip, The Boothill Saloon, which is known for its famous saying, "You're better off here than across the street." Which is a cemetery.

The "pop-ups" consist of an RV converted to a kitchen, twelve folding tables, several sets of chairs, and whatever ambiance the restaurant can create. Each restaurant supports a different charity. Based on our location, traffic for our pop-up should be good, and fifty percent of all proceeds will go to the Epilepsy Fund for Families at Orlando Children's Hospital. It was this foundation that covered a lot of my son's medical bills when my ex-husband's insurance didn't.

Along with my friends, Josie, Paisley, and Jayne, I signed up to work a four-hour shift. Our plan is to hang out afterward and maybe go dancing. Soon, Paisley will get married and move across the world to Japan, since that's where her fiancé Hank's next duty station is.

Good news. I totally need a night out with my friends.

Bad news. They'll instantly see right through me and know something's wrong.

I pull into the designated parking lot for our pop-up, a block east from The Fox and Hound pop up, and check my reflection in my rearview mirror. My eyes are red and puffy from unshed tears, and my throat is splotchy from holding back my angst. Trouble with being a pale-skinned blonde is that all emotion shows on me one way or another. Usually in this blotchy, unflattering way.

I freshen up my mascara, add more blush, and pink my lips with a shiny gloss.

Once my face is back on, I tighten my ponytail, let the few loose strands stay, and force my mouth into a smile. Standing outside my car, I tuck my white T-shirt into the front of my jeans. I've worn my Sketchers because, for me, comfort wins over sexy every time.

The walk is quick, and I come up behind the converted RV that's the kitchen. Jayne is outside the door to the RV, gesturing to staff, likely instructing them on what t their role is. Josie and Paisley flank her side. The restaurant seating takes up most of the parking lot. Several retractable rope-style barricades separate the restaurant patrons from the hundreds of people milling up and down the sidewalk, some drunk as skunks.

Jayne's the first to notice me. She gives me a wink and a smile which I return. Josie and Paisley each give me a wave.

Jayne's my boss at her shop *The Daily Mirror.* I've often heard that people shouldn't go into business with or work for their friends, but Jayne's been a godsend. Her shop hours have given me the flexibility to prioritize Tyler and college.

Jayne gestures for me to hurry to her, and when I'm beside her, she wraps her arm around my shoulder and gives me a side hug.

She says excitedly, "Here she is, our soon to be teacher."

Anything she says always sounds wonderful because of her lovely British accent. Jayne has always, always, always been the cheerleader in my life.

Her support makes me want to whine. I shove those emotions away, something I'm good at.

I say, "Okay! What's the plan? I'm ready. Let's do this. Let's earn some money for epilepsy." I clasp my hands together in forced eagerness, ready to throw myself into the work and forget my troubles for a while.

"Right." Jayne side-eyes me but moves into hostess mode. "The restaurant is divided into four parts. Back left, back right, front left, front right."

Four a-frame signs with our restaurant name and the charity we support are spaced out by the barriers for the passersby.

Jayne continues, "Each section has three tables. Josie is covering the front right. Heather, you'll cover the front left. Paisley and I will cover the backs, and I'll also rotate through, helping where I can. The more people we move through here, the more money we make."

I say, "I love the sound of that."

Josie smiles. "Me too, because Brinn and I have decided to match however much is made here tonight."

Tears spring to my eyes. "Josie, that's so generous." I dab at the corners of my eyes to keep from messing up my makeup.

She shrugs nonchalantly. "We saw how helpful the foundation was to you and Tyler. It's the least we can do." She hands me a napkin. "No crying. We've got money to make."

Paisley, a pretty redhead with a bright smile, pumps her fist. "Let's do this."

I wrap her in a hug. She's in the throes of planning a wedding and getting ready to move overseas, but put all that on hold to do this today.

"Thanks for being here," I say.

She rolls her eyes. "Are you kidding me? Here is the one place I want to be. I want to get as much friend time in as possible. Besides, between working on the wedding with my mom, my sister, and his sister, Gigi, I'm ready to elope. I need to do something other than wedding planning."

Josie puts her fist in the middle of our circle. "Here's to a night where big money is raised, laughter is shared, and good things go down." She wags her brows. "You can take that however you want," she adds with a wicked smile.

We all laugh.

From the pile, three hands with sparkling engagement rings glisten, reflecting the afternoon light. Mine is the only ringless hand. I glance at both Paisley and Jayne. When I was getting my divorce, they were hooking up with their Mr. Wonderfuls. In reflection, I've come a long way. Yeah, it's been hard, but I've done it. And I'll get over this next bump, too.

I squeeze my hand over theirs. "Don't forget to thank everybody for being here, for helping such a good foundation, and push appetizers and desserts."

"Family on three," Josie says.

It reminds me of a football huddle and my early college days when life was classes, football, and easier times.

"One, two, three," Josie says.

"Family," we say in unison and dissolve in laughter because it's fun and silly.

Jayne nods to the rope being removed from our entrance to allow customers in. "Doors are open," she says with air quotes. "I'll start seating people."

There's a line of bikers in all shapes and sizes. Some with long hair, some with short. White-collar or blue-collar, at Bike Week, none of the specifics matter. The only requirement is a love for motorcycles. And often leather.

Jayne seats people, and we're off taking orders. I'm dropping my first order at the counter for Jeff, the cook, when Josie sidles up next to me.

She says, "Wanna tell me what had you looking so blotchy when you arrived?"

I feign ignorance. "The sun?"

She shakes her head. "Wanna try again? I wasn't the only one who noticed. Jayne mentioned it, too."

I blow out a heavy sigh and gesture to the event. "I tried calling you earlier. After all this is over, I need some professional advice."

"Sorry, I haven't had time to check my phone. I was helping with the setup." She raises one brow and looks confused. "Is it that snake of an ex of yours again?"

"If only it were that easy. I need a criminal attorney. Unless you think you might be able to handle it." I look away. I despise asking for help on big-ticket items. Reminds me of how independent I'm not.

Josie was grabbing menus when I dropped the bomb. She slaps them on the counter and faces me. "Spill. Just know that everything you tell me now is considered client-attorney privileges, so if you killed Justin —"

"I need my record expunged. Something stupid I did in college."

She looks slightly disappointed, and gestures for me to continue.

I tell her the sunbathing sorority sister story. I was sick of it. "They dropped the charges and all thirteen of us paid a fine, so I'm surprised I have a record."

"Because you were arrested, you have a record."

I nod. "Is it possible to have my record expunged?"

She does a slight side nod. "Anything's possible."

"Is it possible to have it expunged by Tuesday?"

Josie lets out a low whistle. "I'm not going to say yes or no. Let me do some research, and I'll know for sure first thing tomorrow. In the meantime, don't panic."

"Easy for you to say. Expunging starts at a grand. Which I'll reimburse." I take the plates off the counter as I prepare to deliver them. She grabs the extra plates and follows me.

"I won't take it, and if we need to get outside help, I can cover that."

"I won't take a handout." We pause our conversation while we deliver the plates and ask if the patrons need anything else.

On our way back to the counter, Josie says, "It's not a handout. It's a loan."

I shake my head. "I can take care of myself. I have it in savings."

"I know you can. You're awesome at it. And that money in savings is to cover living expenses while you do your student teaching. You can't survive on love and air."

"But if it takes time to clear the record, then I might be able to save up the money again while I wait for the next round of student teaching assignments."

Josie says, "My offer is always on the table. I know you have other things going on, like your dishwasher being out. I don't want you to be spread too thin. We've all been there."

Only, she really hasn't. She was born with a silver spoon in her mouth and married a man who became a self-made millionaire. Josie's always had a safety net.

"Thanks, but like I said, I pay my debts."

She shrugs. "Whatever you say." She kisses me on the forehead. "Now, go fix your face because you have red lips on your forehead."

I groan and walk into the RV to use the chrome-plated microwave as a mirror to do as she says. Afterward, the afternoon moves into the evening in a blur. The pop-up restaurant is a hit with steady business. I let myself forget about my problems and enjoy my time with my friends.

There's an hour left to my shift when Jayne comes up to me at the serving counter.

She says, "I just sat four hot guys in your section. Go over there and dazzle them into buying lots of appetizers and drinks. Not alcoholic, mind you, they're on bikes, but let's make some last money for epilepsy and go out with a bang."

I give her two thumbs up. "You got it." I freshen my lipstick, but mostly because my lips are chapped. I like that colored Chapstick that makes you feel like you're not wearing lipstick but gives just the right pop of color. I pull my ponytail tighter, grab four menus from the counter, and stroll over to the table.

Two of the guys are facing me and two have their backs to me. They're broad, solid men, built like lumberjacks but without the beards. Two are African American, one with dreads, and two are white, one sporting a sleeve of tattoos on both arms. They're dressed in jeans and T-shirts, and carrying leather jackets or vests.

"Good evening, gentlemen," I say as I deal out the menus like a deck of cards. "Welcome to the Fox and Hound. Your choosing to dine with us is a big deal because fifty percent of your tab will be donated to the Epilepsy Fund for Families at Orlando Children's Hospital. This fund helps offset medical costs not covered by insurance. The last thing parents need to worry about is whether their child's treatment will be covered. Everything you eat and drink tonight is for a good cause. This is not the time to be on a diet. This is the time to indulge, because why not? You're helping families of kids with epilepsy." I make a point of smiling at each one of them.

Until I get to the fourth guy. My heart stutters in my chest, causing shortness of breath, making me cough as I try to take in air. This sensation is a familiar one. It's the first sign of a panic attack. My heart races, and I feel light-headed. I didn't recognize him earlier because his back was to me. And I wasn't expecting to see him again, ever.

"Heather?" he says with his green eyes shining. His smile is wide and welcoming. "It's been years."

Nine years to be exact. I'm reminded of this every March when conversations and news outlets start talking about the NFL draft. The draft is, after all, the reason why I broke up with Dax Griffin.

No one wants to be the girl left behind when the guy she's been dating gets drafted and moves on to bigger and better things. And what guy would keep the unremarkable small-town girl they'd only been dating for six months when supermodels and the like were about to become part of his lifestyle? I was determined to be the dumper and not the dumpee.

CHAPTER 4
FRIDAY

I'M SPEECHLESS. I BREATHE IN DEEPLY THROUGH MY NOSE, grappling for control, trying not to have a freak-out panic attack in front of Dax Griffin. Holy Lord.

He's as gorgeous today as he was back then. Still boyishly handsome with light brown sun-streaked hair cut close and the one dimple in his right cheek. A scar runs from the corner of his left eye to his temple, created by a cleat and a collision on the field his senior year. I was there.

Sweet Jesus, I had it bad for him. And, for a while, I did have him. He was mine, and I was his, and it was beautiful and easy and everything you imagine a relationship to be. There was fun and laughter. He was a friend and a lover. Our brief time together was oh-so-good.

Then he was marked for a high draft pick. More importantly, Dax knew he had the attention of several professional teams and was likely going to a team across the country. I know this because my brother explained how the draft worked, and the first three teams up were west coast teams. Followed by two northern teams.

I asked Dax once what he thought would happen, and he'd said we'd know on draft day. I got that; I did. What I didn't get was how we never even had a hypothetical conversation. All this let me think our six months together meant more to me than him. Pair that with his over-the-top excitement about his future and no mention of my place in it and, well, I just did the expected.

"Dax," I say in a strangled whisper. "Wow, what are the odds of running into you after all these years?"

Not that it mattered because the unthinkable had just happened.

He pushes from his chair and comes around the table to embrace me in a hug.

Never in a million years did I ever imagine seeing Dax again. Some people dream about running into a former boyfriend. I never did. I imagined it would feel humiliating.

I imagined correctly.

But seriously, what are the odds? I suppose I could ask Jayne's man Stacy. He's a math genius and would know the odds in a second.

"Who cares?" Dax says after stepping back slightly. "It's fantastic running into you. You look great."

Nine years in the league, one too many concussions, and he retired. I had hoped he'd stayed on the west coast. And yeah, I checked his Instagram occasionally. There wasn't any mention of an east coast visit. His parents were in Tampa since his dad was the head coach for the pro team there. Which is why I avoid Tampa.

Today, I think I'd be justified in saying the universe has been quite the dick to me. Seriously. First my school and so-called criminal record, and now my old flame from college shows up. The one I never really got over.

"You look great, too." I nod to emphasize my point while I scan for an escape. Man, I was so head-over-heels for him. Probably why I was overly sensitive to his sudden fame. Who could compete with that?

Ending things made my heart feel as if it had been stomped on by Dax's stupid football cleats. And that old ache revisits me now. I don't really want to stand here and make small talk.

He says, "I heard you married and had a kid. You have just the one, or more? I'm assuming you stayed in town close to your folks."

I grew up in Daytona. He grew up everywhere, since his dad worked for whatever team hired him. He attended the University of Central Florida on a full football scholarship. I attended it on the student loan plan.

"Just the one." Then a lie slips off my tongue like melted butter. "I have a house over on the beach." I point in the direction of Josie's place. Not that we could see it from here on Main Street.

Dax left college and, if his Instagram account is an accurate storyteller, has a fabulous life, including nice homes, vacations, and expensive cars. I'll be damned if I would be someone he pities because my life has turned out the polar opposite of his.

"Wow, the beach. Nice. I like the sound of the ocean as white noise. I had a place near water in Cali, too." His attempt to connect fell flat. "Sounds like you and your husband are doing well." He glances at my ring finger. My bare ring finger. I hocked the diamond to pay for auto repairs.

I shrug nonchalantly. "I don't have any complaints."

"Did you end up getting your psych degree?"

Clearly, he didn't track me to the same degree I had him.

I choke on air. "Would you believe I went into fashion? I co-own a shop in town. A high-end boutique. We have a big online presence." Another lie. I work *for* Jayne, not with her, but maybe she'd pretend otherwise in case he asks.

He gives both of my shoulders an affectionate squeeze. "I knew you'd do great things. You're just that sort of person."

Humiliation sets in. I can feel the red heat creeping up my neck, and Dax knows this is my tell. He used to dog me about it. There's a chance he could've forgotten, but not likely, the way my luck is going today.

"Thanks. So how about I give you guys time to look at the menu and think about what you want to order?"

But Dax is relentless as ever. "I don't want to lose touch. I miss our friendship. If your husband's good with it, how about I give you guys some tickets to a few of the games in Tampa? I know the coach." He elbows me in that ha-ha, I'm kidding way. "Is your husband a football fan?"

I shake my head. "Not really, Golf." Golf was Justin's mistress during our marriage. But he'd sell his mom for football tickets. Tyler would be over the moon excited as well.

I step back. "Have a seat. Look at the menu. Spend lots of money." Then I take a second step backward. I need to get away before Dax sees my embarrassment. It's not like I can say it was a sudden sunburn.

"I'll check back with you all in a bit," I say, picking up my backward pace. My white T-shirt will only highlight my new splotchiness. In my haste, I narrowly avoid colliding with Paisley and knocking the tray from her hands.

"Sorry," I mumble as I scurry to the kitchen. I hide out of sight and begin the litany of self-talk I use to calm myself when Tyler's hospitalized. If it worked then, it can work now.

Jayne finds me, her brow furrowed in concern. "What has you bothered?"

I alternate between fanning myself with my hand and tugging my shirt back and forth to cool my neck.

"Oh, my Lord, Jayne. In college, I dated one of the guys at my corner table."

Her brows shoot up. "Oh, is that good or bad? Can we pick good?"

I groan. "No, it's not good. He went on to fulfill his life's dream. He's since dated supermodels."

Jayne's shoulders straighten. "What's this bloke's name? Remember when you got drunk at Josie's wedding and called out a name?"

I glare at her. "*No,* I don't remember. I was drunk."

"I do. When Doug carted you off, you said something about a Max or—" She taps her temple in thought. "What was the name?"

"Dax?" I say with hesitation. Had I really said his name?

She points at me. "That's it."

I point at the table. "That's him."

Jayne's eyes go wide. "Bugger." She purses her lips in brief thought then says, "You need to get out there and show him how fabulous you are." She drags me to the bar. "Here, take some frosted mugs and a pitcher to them and tell them it's on the house."

I shake my head. "You take it." I point to my red rashy-looking chest.

Jayne puts the pitcher of beer she'd just filled on the counter. "Heather, listen to me, love. You're more than the girl he loved and left. You're a fabulous mum. You're a fighter. You're brave and strong and independent. We all see that. Why can't you?"

Because I'm not any of those things yet, I want to say. Because I'm trying to be, but when I think I've found my strength in one, I'm reminded by life how I'm failing in another.

"I'll give you ten dollars to take my table," I propose.

She takes my tray then loads it with the pitcher of beer and four mugs. "Is he dating anyone?"

I shake my head. "Last I saw, he and his model girlfriend broke up. Not that they dated all that long. Maybe six weeks of Instagram posts, and then I noticed she stopped following him."

A smile plays at the corner of Jayne's mouth. "Is that so? Well, then go out there and make him wonder why he ever let you go."

I slide the tray onto my hand, balancing it. "And how am I supposed to do that in the few seconds we interact?"

"By being your magnificent self." She cocks her head as a way to tell me to move.

I count to twenty and get control of my breathing before I square my shoulders and decide she's right. I glide over to the table, digging deep for confidence. I once read a book that talked about adopting an alter ego as a means to get through challenging situations. If I had to pick one for tonight, it would be Wonder Woman. Though a sex kitten type was likely what most people would pick, I would never be comfortable enough to pull that off.

"Hey guys," I say as I lower the tray to the table. "Beer is on the house while you look at the menu. I'm guessing y'all are on bikes so you'll notice our frosty mugs are smaller than typical. We encourage the one drink maximum for your safety." Part of the tray is resting against the side of my hip as I unload the mugs, the other part against the table. Dax is to my right so I position myself to be facing him.

Jayne's right. I can totally pull this off. If I keep my interactions to short bursts, I can be funny and flirty and totally a badass like Wonder Woman. I don't have to be down-on-her-luck Heather.

I reach across my body to deliver the next mug to Dax and pair it with a bright smile. With a cute flick of my hand, I send the mug sliding the remaining distance toward Dax. It's a trick Josie taught me.

Dax smiles back, staring into my eyes, and leans across the table to catch the mug while I reach for another mug for his friend. This offsets the table's balance and pops my side of the table up as his weight pushes his side down.

The table see-sawing while I hand off a mug means I can't grab my tray in time to stabilize it. And, in what feels like slow motion, the pitcher of beer is bucked toward me, sending it colliding with my chest, spilling its contents down my front. The tray and pitcher clatter to the floor.

Gasping in surprise from the cold brew, I jump back and collide with the person at the table beside Dax's, who just happens to be standing up at the same time. The impact of our collision bounces me sideways.

"I'm so sorry," I say as I attempt to pull the clingy white T-shirt from my chest. Reflex has me looking down at my clothes to assess the damage. At that moment, my feet get tangled, I twist, and lose my balance. As I fall, I windmill my arms hoping the action will magically help me regain my balance. As if.

But momentum has control and tosses me backward into the straps connecting the stanchions that are our restaurant's perimeter. Beyond the barricade is the sidewalk, crowds of people, and motorcycles and occasional cars going up and down the street. As is common during Bike Week, bikers, many of who are patrons of the pop-up restaurants, have parked their motorcycles on the sidewalk to keep them out of the road.

The trajectory of my fall has me landing on a blood-red Harley Davidson Sportster with a tank painted with black skulls and crossbones.

The momentum from my impact pushes the skull and crossbones bike into the one next to it, and like a series of dominoes, four bikes parked in the row drop to their sides, one onto the other in a cacophony of metal colliding with metal.

I land with a yelp and roll to my side, horrified. Sharp pain shoots through my upper leg where the motorcycle's chrome foot peg jammed into my hip. I swear it touched bone. My first thought? Odds were good that one of the four owners of the knocked down bikes was going to kill me. So now would be a perfect time to die from embarrassment.

CHAPTER 5
FRIDAY

CALL ME CHICKEN, BUT WITH THE WAY MY DAY WAS GOING, I didn't want to stick around and get my ass handed to me by a biker.

Wincing but pushing back the pain, I spring up and scan the crowd. Sure enough, Josie's running interference. She's in front of a group of bikers with long hair and nothing but leather clothes kept together with chains. A hulk-sized one with tattoos running up both arms is pointing a finger at me like a person might point a knife. I could be exaggerating that, but I'm not mistaking the angry look on his face. Dax has jumped into the conversation with Josie and the bikers.

Because I landed outside the stanchions, I can easily be absorbed into the crowd. I pull myself up and eye my escape route, the quickest path to my van, which now feels like I've parked it one million miles away.

Looking back at the restaurant crowd, and I see Jayne rushing toward me, my purse in her hand. Behind her, Dax's friends are picking up the bikes I knocked over.

"Are you okay?" she asks as she presses my purse into my chest, covering my see-through shirt and booby area.

Because, yeah, I'd worn a T-shirt bra, and now everyone has been gifted with x-ray vision and can see through my shirt.

"Other than I want to die from mortification? Yeah, I guess so."

"I assumed you wouldn't want to stay."

Over her shoulder, Dax moves away from the bikers and toward me. He gives me a thumbs up.

The long-haired biker yells across the parking-lot-turned-restaurant to me, "Don't you worry about anything, pretty lady, and I hope they figure out why you have those muscle spasms."

I glance from Jayne to the guy then smile and do a small wave because I don't know what to say.

Jayne shakes her head and says under her breath, "It's anyone's guess what Josie told him."

I say to Jayne, "If there's damages, will you let me know?"

She shakes her head. "No, because you've got enough on your plate."

"Heather?" Dax says, having come up behind Jayne.

Jayne's eyes go big.

I fake smile and rapid blink to keep from making eye contact. "Dax, this is my friend Jayne. Jayne, this is Dax. We went to college together."

Jayne swivels and goes into her work-the-customer mode.

"Dax, it's lovely to meet you." She puts my purse behind her back.

I take it and attempt to slip away. More like limp away. My hip and leg throb, and putting weight on them is excruciating. With my day, I wouldn't be surprised if I broke something.

"Heather," Dax calls.

But I keep going, putting the restaurant behind me and doing my best to blend into the biker crowd that fills the streets. Thankfully, a girl covered in beer doesn't stand out in this crowd.

I push through a hodgepodge of motorcycle buffs dressed in ensembles that would make the men of Queer Eye faint in horror.

As I make my way toward my minivan and away from the restaurant, I begin to breathe easier, believing I'm home free. From seemingly nowhere—yes, I kept checking over my shoulder—Dax appears and pulls me to a stop by tugging at my elbow.

I yelp in pain as the movement pulls me sideways and requires me to put more weight on my injured side. He releases my elbow with a flurry of apologies. I shift and hop on my uninjured leg, giving my hurt side a break.

"I was going to ask if you're okay, but I can see that you aren't." He frowns down at me.

People swarm around us. We're like two fish blocking the flow of a stream as we've stopped in the middle of the sidewalk.

"I'm fine. Really. What was it you used to say when one of the other players got hurt on the field? Just rub some dirt on it? That's what I'll do. It'll be fine." I try not to wince as throbbing aches course through me.

"You're not fine. Let me call your husband. He should come and get you and take you to the emergency room or something."

I shake my head. "That won't be necessary."

"How about I get one of your friends to take you?"

Someone bumps me, and I grit my teeth to keep from showing any discomfort.

Dax rolls his eyes and leans toward me. "On three, I'm going to move you out of the way. Ready?"

"Wait, what?"

"One, two, three." He wraps his arms around my waist and lifts me up so that my boobs are slightly below his chin. I bet I smell *great*. Like beer and sweat. Every man's dream.

He's gentle as he moves me off the sidewalk into a small alcove against a building. We're still in the thick of things, but no longer in anyone's way. He lowers me ever so slowly, like I'm floating on a cloud, and leans me up against the building.

"Which friend do you want me to go back and get?"

"They can't leave. They'll be too shorthanded to run the restaurant, and the money is for a good cause."

"You're a good cause, too. If you won't let me get one of them, then give me your phone." He puts his hand out expectedly.

"Why?"

"I'm going to call your husband."

"Nope," I say. "I'll drive home and can take care of everything when I get there."

"If you don't give me your phone, I'm going to track him down myself on my phone." He slips his phone out of his back pocket and begins to do what I assume is scrolling and keying in something in a search engine.

I put my hand over his phone. "Stop, Dax. Please." I don't want to tell him the truth.

"Why don't you want him to come help you? That's what a partner is for."

I have two options. I can continue with the lie and maybe get away with it. Or maybe I'll dig myself in deeper. Or…

"Because we're divorced," I whisper.

A beat of silence passes.

Dax nods his head twice. "Good, that'll make this easier."

"What?"

"Count of three," he says and begins counting.

"What?"

On three, he bends over and scoops me up, carrying me like a groom does a bride when they're about to cross over the threshold. I clench my teeth, not from the pain this time, but sheer determination not to get lost in the memories of our time together and the what-ifs that are sure to follow.

"Where's your car?"

Mutely, I point in the direction. "I'm getting your clothes wet." It's the only thing I can think to say. Our faces are so close, and everything about him is familiar.

"Who cares," he says.

I've heard people talk about muscle memory. Is that the same as body memory? Because my body remembers Dax's. Nestling up against him brings back a host of wonderful memories. Kinda like when you hear that one song or catch a whiff of a certain smell, and the memory overcomes you. If my shirt wasn't sopping wet and clinging to my skin, if my hip wasn't throbbing, this would be a great moment. A sexy one. A moment I'd consider letting myself get lost in. After all, two years have passed since I was last naked with a man. And here is a gorgeous one who smells like sandalwood with a hint of vanilla and…hops? Nope, that's me.

But one truth holds me back.

Having an entanglement of any sort with Dax would be stupid. Getting over him had taken what felt like a lifetime, and I can't go through that again. Not that he's even propositioned me.

Briefly, I let myself enjoy being close to him, savoring the short, wonderful fantasy.

"I don't mind carrying you, but if we're coming up to your car anytime soon, you might want to give me a heads up. If we were headed toward the beach instead of away, I'd assume I was carrying you to your house."

I startle and put my focus on my surroundings. We'd gone twenty feet past my mom-mobile. My worn-out minivan. Definitely not the vehicle of a successful person.

I point over his shoulder, behind us. "It's back there. But you can drop me here, and I'll be good."

He shakes his head. "Nope. I'm going to drive you home or to the emergency room. I'll let you pick." He does an about-face and walks toward the parking lot.

"Mine is the minivan. The blue one." As if the lot is overrun with minivans. Mine is the only one. I almost add, "With the damaged front panel," but why point out the obvious?

"Don't take this wrong, but you're the minivan type."

"Every woman in the world would take that wrong," I say.

"Well, you shouldn't because you're the kind of girl that runs a mean carpool, the mom who brings the best snacks, and has a minivan full of kids."

"You mean the worn-out-looks-harried mom?" I'd long given up trying to compete with the stay-at-home moms. Not that they asked to compete, but I gave myself permission not to do it. Life was too busy for me to sweat those things.

"No, I mean the hot mom that looks good doing everything. She's the dream, watching her slide out of the minivan with her tight jeans and ponytail. Every guy's dream."

"Except yours," I say without thinking.

He stops walking and lowers me to the ground. We've reached my van.

"We were kids, Heather. Yeah, I was focused on building my foundation for the long-term."

"You sound like your dad," I said. Because this was the repeated message from his dad. "Don't get serious," he'd tell me, "Dax has big plans that don't include settling down."

I blew him off. Secretly questioning how well he knew his kid when I was the one sleeping with him. Didn't that mean I knew him better?

Guess not. Because when Dax was making career and life choices, I wasn't invited into the conversation.

"Let's not argue, please." He sighs heavily. "I love that we've run into each other. I want this to be a good memory."

As if spilling beer all over myself and knocking down motorcycles could be a good memory for me.

"Thanks for getting me to my car. I can take it from here." Truth is, I need him to walk away. I need to get into my minivan and have a good cry. Part of me *wants* him to take care of me. Part of me *wants* him to make sure I get home safely and that nothing is wrong with my hip or leg. It's been forever since a man has done that for me. And maybe I shouldn't want a man to take care of me, maybe feminists everywhere would revolt, but a partner would be glorious. And in my case, that partner would be a man.

But even if I were to give in, I wouldn't dare give in to Dax. That would be just plain stupid.

I'll end this day on a positive, for him at least. "I'm glad you sat at my table tonight. I'm not glad that I knocked over four bikes or that my hip is throbbing something awful. But seeing you again is... nice." That's true, but if I'm given a do-over, I'm not sure I'd keep the running into him in the picture.

"Nice? Huh. No one's ever said that to me."

I snort-laugh. "Oh, I'm sure you've had a lot of smoke blown up your butt since you entered the NFL."

He chuckles and holds out his hand, palm up. "I guess that's probably true. I think I might have become desensitized to it. Or accustomed to it. Because you saying seeing me again is 'nice' doesn't feel all that good."

I point to his hand. "What do you want me to do with this? And I'm not going to stroke your ego. Nice is all I got."

He jiggles his hand. "I want your keys."

"Dax, I need to end the night here."

His gaze meets mine and he holds it, then searches my face. A small, slight smile crooks up one side of his mouth. He drops his hand and says, "Okay, I guess I'm just so happy to see you I don't want it to end."

I appreciate his candor. It's refreshing, even if it's a line.

"How about we end on a nice gesture?"

He smirks. "There's that word 'nice' again."

I point to his damp shirt. "Considering I've already left my mess on you, how about we say goodbye with a hug?"

Not that I think contact is a good idea, but it seems like a fitting goodbye. And it would be a better end than the time we broke up. I believe I slapped his face and then burst into tears. Dax was my prince charming, unknowingly setting the bar so high, in hindsight I wonder if no other man had a chance.

He lifts a damp lock of hair from my neck. "I know you said you wouldn't give me your keys, but if I don't make sure you get home okay and aren't in need of medical attention, I won't be able to live with myself."

"How about I text you when I get home and then again in the morning to prove I'm okay. It's the best I can offer," I say.

He appears to consider it for a moment then holds out his hand. "Hand me your phone, and I'll put my number in."

I dig through my purse and do as he asks. While he's putting in his information, I unlock my van and toss my purse inside.

He hands me my phone. "Promise you'll text?"

I shrug. "Sure, unless I'm dead."

His eyes narrow.

I laugh. "Okay, terrible joke. Sorry."

His frowny face is cute. "So, this is it?" he says.

I nod.

He opens his arms. "Come here. I'll take that hug now. We have too much history for anything less. Don't you think?" Dax side-eyes me. "Unless you're afraid a hug from me might make you fall head-over-heels."

"Puh-lease, I spent six months with you and never fell head-over-heels. I doubt one little hug will do me in." All lies. Maybe I'm trying to rewrite history. Maybe I want him to think differently about the time we spent together and wonder if he misread it, too.

Dax opens his arms wider, as if possible, and steps closer. "Then bring it in, Lowell." His arms drop slightly as he says, "Wait, that's not your last name anymore. What is it?"

"Michaels." I haven't been Heather Lowell in years. That girl was curious and adventurous. That girl sunbathed topless on a roof. Heather Michaels is serious and cautious. She wears sunscreen at night.

I step into his arms and, keeping at least an inch between

us, give him what I'd call a casual hug. One without real meaning.

He wraps his arms around me bear-hug style and crushes me against him. "Man, running into you made my day. You were the one positive constant in college while I chased my football dreams."

He sounds wistful.

"Do you regret pursuing an NFL career?" Especially knowing now what it cost his health.

"I didn't at the time or while I was in it, but now, on the other side…" he trails off.

I'm tucked under his head. My wet shirt and chest press against his solid one. His hug is so encompassing I feel sheltered from the world. He's got me. My entire weight is against him and I'm fully supported. I exhale and let someone else carry me, if only for a moment.

"On the other side of what? You're older? You wish you were somewhere else in your life? What?" My words come out faint with my face against his chest. I can't imagine his life being too hard. Sure, a football schedule is tough, grueling. But he's well compensated. Money can't buy everything, but comfort is a wonderful place to start.

"Are my early thirties too soon for a midlife crisis?" He chuckles, and the deepness of his laugh reverberates against me.

"Yes." I return the laugh. Then I'm pulled back in time to the game we used to play, a game I still play. "If you had one wish, right now, what would it be? You remember the rules. It can't be for more wishes."

We started this game as a lark, as a way to get what we wanted. Usually sex. But sometimes, when drinking, it would become philosophical.

Dax snuggles into me, not letting go of the hug, and I rest against him. Part of me says, what harm can this do? Another smarter part of me tsks and shakes her head at me.

"Ah, man. I haven't thought of this in a long time." He strokes my head. "My one wish would be to make the most of this moment. I spent so much time trying to get to the next milestone that I forgot to enjoy the now. And right now, I'm enjoying the hell out of this."

Me, too. And I know I shouldn't be. But I am. And I want more. More of this moment right now.

CHAPTER 6
FRIDAY

Maybe it's because the day was so stinking awful. Maybe it's because Dax's hug comes when I need one the most. Even though I totally embarrassed myself in front of him. But that doesn't seem to matter. Right here, right now, I don't want this moment to end. I don't want to go home with a bruised and aching hip to a dishwasher that doesn't work, a toilet that runs off and on, a yard that needs mowing, and the host of other issues that will greet me in the morning.

I want to be Heather Lowell one last time. Heather Lowell who only has to think about today.

I ask, "What was one thing about our time together you remember the most."

He says without hesitation, "We laughed a lot. All the time. I can't even remember why we laughed sometimes, but we did."

"Yeah," I say. "We did. Usually some competition we'd dream up." I worked at the gym where Dax and the team worked out, and I'd always challenge him to some silly race or weightlifting reps.

"Or sex," Dax says. "We laughed a lot while having sex."

I pushed away in mock annoyance. "Not during sex. Before and after sex." My keys are in my hand, so I press the unlock and the back-passenger door open button without looking. "There was nothing funny about our sex."

Dax tosses his head back and laughs. "No, but it sure was fun. We found some creative places to, ahem, connect."

I pitch my purse in the van along with my keys and sit on the floor, my back resting partly against the seat. I stretch my leg and aching hip, rubbing the spot where I hit the foot peg.

"Yeah, I'm not sure I had an ounce of modesty back then. Now, I'm horrified to think about all those places. It was a miracle we weren't ever caught."

He kneels by my leg, pushes my hand away, and takes over the massage. "I've had plenty of injuries in my day. I'm good at massages." He kneads the area.

And I moan with relief. "Man, that feels good."

"It's all about getting to that muscle belly. That's where the muscle fibers can be tapped." He taps the length of the muscle that runs along my outer leg, then goes back to the center of it and rubs his thumb into the muscle.

I shift so I can lean back. I reach under the passenger seat, the one where my kid's booster seat is latched to, and pull up on the adjuster handle to scoot the seat back and give me more room.

Dax peers into the back of the van. "Wow, these have lots of space."

"There's a third row there, but I keep it down to haul all sorts of things but mainly groceries." I had to haul Tyler's sleep monitor last week since his doctor is doing a sleep study to assess if seizures happen at night. I also keep blankets,] a bin of food, and water for emergencies. I'm ever the practical person these days.

"I think this van is badass." He rubs my upper thigh and looks at me.

In the dim beam of my van's interior light, our eyes meet. His hand rests on my leg and my relaxed body tenses as a surge of sexual need shoots through me. I'd love for his hand to roam, and I hate myself for wanting it so badly.

His thumb strokes small circles on my thigh. "If I had one wish, I'd wish for one more night with you."

For the longest time after we broke up, I had that same wish. Sex wasn't the only thing I missed about Dax; more the easy companionship we shared.

And sitting here, talking with him, his hand on my leg, only emphasizes how lonely I've been. A person can get hugged by their family or child, but it's different from being hugged by a man who's sexually interested. Inside me, something sparks to life. It's a part that's been on hold for a long time. Neglected and lonely.

I lean forward so our faces are close. "We have right now. Right here. This van. Just you and me."

He holds my gaze. "Heather, that's not a funny joke."

"It's not a joke. This may sound crazy, but I want to be Heather Lowell again. Just for a few hours."

"Like Cinderella with a glass slipper."

"Only I don't mind going back to my kid. He's awesome. But right now, I'd like to be more than someone's mom."

"You're the hottest mom I've ever seen. Especially with how that shirt clings to your chest. Makes it hard for a man to look you in the eyes. All those guys on the street were checking you out. I was glad your hurt leg gave me an excuse to carry you."

"You don't have to flatter me, Dax. I'm a sure thing tonight, but if you keep talking, I might change my mind."

He shuffles forward on his knees slowly until his lips are a hint from mine. "I think I can shut up long enough to kiss you."

His hand slides up my thigh and around to my backside, cupping my butt. He slides me forward to meet him and when our bodies connect, the air between us sizzles.

I'm going to embrace this experience with no regrets. This moment, this bliss, is all mine.

His kiss begins soft as he explores and relearns me. Because it's been awhile, the first touch is almost foreign, but moments later the novel is replaced with familiar. I know this man, his lips, his taste. We slip into the past and know without having to ask what the other likes.

"Where can we take this?" Dax mumbles against my lips.

With his shirt fisted in my hand, I draw him into the van. "Let's take this to the cargo area?" I say with laughter and a wink.

He clicks the lever to close the door as I low scoot between the middle row seats and into the spacious cargo area. He follows. I flip open one of the spare blankets I keep in the back for Tyler and lie back on it, opening myself up to Dax.

He hovers over me, and I see his smile in the moonlight. "I think I might be too tall; my feet touch the back of the driver's seat." His legs extend back between the two captain chairs of the middle row.

"All the better to brace yourself," I say wickedly.

He laughs while lifting the hem of my T-shirt. "Let's get this wet shirt off you."

It's a flurry of shirts coming off and jeans sliding down.

We bump our heads against each other and the top of the van, but I don't care, and I can tell Dax doesn't either. His single focus is on me. Like I'm the center of the universe. And I revel in this adoration.

"Heather, are you sure you're good with this here? We can go back to my room, or we can—"

"Are you gonna use that mouth to yammer all night, or is there something better you can do with it?" Because here is perfect. If we leave, I'll second-guess everything. This is living in the moment.

Dax cups my cheek and says, "Let me show you what I can do." He softly drops on top of me and proceeds to show me his skills.

Setting doesn't matter. All that counts is that we are in each other's arms. We caress and explore once-familiar land. He kisses my cesarean scar. When we join, I cling to him as I shudder and release and then hold him tightly when he does the same.

Afterward, I rest against him, his large hand stroking my hair. He kisses my temple.

"I have a cramp in my injured leg," I say with regret. Because I don't want to pop the bubble.

"I can help with that," he says and rolls me over. He straddles me then claps his hands together with a solid smack. He rubs them vigorously as if to warm them then presses one palm to my bruised hip and the other to the inner thigh on the same leg.

"Let me show you a few things I learned since we last connected," he says.

"Mood killer," I say. "No woman wants to hear about a guy's other conquests, especially after having rocking sex in her shaggin' wagon."

"Oh, this isn't about other conquests. And I promise. I can get that mood right back."

He proceeds to prove his point. And I'm happily wrong all night long.

CHAPTER 7

FRIDAY

I can't even recall the last time I came home way too late and snuck in quietly. Before college, maybe?

Dax's scent still on my body and a smile on my face, I fall into bed and sleep solid, something I rarely do.

Thankfully, my mother and Tyler were none the wiser as to how I spent my night. Though, as Mom stares at me over morning coffee, I once again feel like a teen who did a whole lot of something she shouldn't have.

"How did last night go?" she says in her sing-song voice.

Tyler's watching cartoons on the couch, eating frozen waffles. Literally frozen, straight from the freezer. I used to make homemade ones, but he prefers these, so he gets them on weekends for a treat.

"Fine. Josie texted this morning and said we made a lot of money for the charity."

Mom gives me two thumbs up. "And afterward, did you have fun? You work so hard, sweetheart. I hope you treated yourself."

I blow on my coffee, a slight smile playing on my lips. "I

did treat myself. I had a wonderful time." And maybe I'll be good for another two years or less if I can get this criminal record thing worked out. How sad I put so much on hold until after I graduate. As if my life only begins once I have my degree. Or maybe it's because I can't juggle all those balls.

Dax and I separated after two in the morning. We didn't exchange promises to keep in touch. I made it clear I had no expectations. Our time together was a one-off. I wanted to pat myself on the back for not falling into some fantasy that more could come from sex in the minivan.

"I'm glad," Mom says. "And so now you can let your father and me treat you. We want to buy you a new dishwasher."

I set down my mug, a tad too hard, and coffee sloshes over the side. "We've had this discussion. I appreciate the offer, but a new dishwasher is a waste of money. It's an issue of parts and labor, and this one can be fixed." I gesture half-heartedly to my dishwasher.

"Then let us pay for that."

"Mom," I say on a sigh. "You already do so much for me with keeping Tyler after school and last night. I can't continue to mooch off you guys for everything else. I still owe you and Dad for the tires on the van."

When Justin and I divorced, the first thing my dad said was how he anticipated Tyler and I would need to move in with him and Mom, and if that were to happen, then we could only stay for two years. He would not have a child of his living with him forever. That's why when Mom offers to pay for something, I know she doesn't tell Dad. I know it's behind his back, and I love her for wanting to help. But I'm not about to put her in a position to have trouble with my father. Who, by the way, when he loaned me money for tires, made me sign a contract with terms, interest, and a payment plan.

"When you're out of school and making steady money, then you can make this argument, but right now is when you should take all the help you can get." Working for Jayne pays better than minimum wage but still lower than an entry-level teacher. Plus, the health insurance with Jayne is costly because she's a small business. Even though Tyler's covered by his dad's insurance, I am not.

I love my mom and her generous heart. I say, "I'll take the money from my savings and have the dishwasher fixed if it means that much to you."

Mom looks horrified. "No, you've been saving for over a year. That money is earmarked for your student teaching."

I smile and put my hand over hers. "Exactly. If the dishwasher was so important, then I would make accommodations for it. But it's not. When I'm working in my field, then I'll take care of the dishwasher. It's just not that important to me right now."

This was my way of putting the conversation in perspective and not hurting her feelings.

She squeezes my hand. "I want to help as much as I can."

"I know, and I appreciate it. It's just me and Ty. We don't make a lot of dirty dishes," I say jokingly because my kid is like a dirt gnome. He can dirty up a kitchen, bathroom, or any room in a matter of seconds. He's a one cup per drink kinda guy, even if the drink is a refill.

My phone rings, catching me off guard. No one calls early in the morning on a weekend unless it's my mother, and she's sitting right across from me.

The screen tells me it's Jayne calling from the shop.

"Hey," I say, wondering if I maybe forgot to do something at the store. My job is to log inventory, photograph it, and send the info to the website manager to put online. I also help with setting up the store, scheduling private clients, and logging whatever I can into her accounting books since Jayne sucks at doing that.

"I'm soooo sorry, Heather," she says in a rush of words.

"For what?"

"Your fella was here. Dax. He was looking for you. Did you tell him you were part owner?"

I groan. "Oh. My. Lord. I'm so sorry—"

In a flurry of words, she says, "Oh, I don't care about that. But I think I might have blown it for you. He came in, said he was looking for the owner. I said I was the owner. He said the other owner, and I said there is no other owner. He said Heather Lowell then corrected himself and said Michaels. And I said, 'Oh, that other owner. She's not in today.' I was totally caught off guard when he didn't ask for you straight off."

My heart is racing. "Then what happened?"

"Oh dear," she says. "I said you were at home, and he asked where that was. I was so flustered trying to cover for you that I told him where you live."

I gasp and stand up, suddenly knocking over my coffee mug, sending the contents across the table and onto the floor. "I think I might be sick."

Jayne rarely gets flustered. If the fact that Dax was on his way to my house wasn't so unsettling, I'd call her on her BS. Likely, she was matchmaking. But right now I have bigger issues.

"How long ago?"

"He just left. If he comes straight away, then you have fifteen minutes."

Holy crap. I needed to get out of here. I didn't want Dax to know where I lived. Fifteen minutes was not enough time to move or get Tyler out of the house. I glanced at my mother and knew she couldn't be trusted to wave Dax off. She'd invite him in and make him breakfast, lunch, and dinner - all the meals until I returned home.

"Heather, what's wrong?" Mom asks as she rushes to the sink to get a towel to mop up my coffee.

My white T-shirt is oversized and stained. My biker shorts are ratty since they're older than my child but comfortable as heck to sleep in. My hair is a tangled mess. Actually, the only thing I did when I came in early this morning was brush my teeth and wash my face. I can't sleep with makeup on; I'm quick to get acne.

I spin in a circle, trying to make a plan. "I have to go," I say to Jayne.

"Do you want me to call in reinforcements? I can't leave the shop but—"

"No, no. I got it. I'll text an SOS if I need one."

"Darling, I know you aren't going to answer the door. But maybe you should. Even if it's to tell him to bugger off and slam it seconds later," Jayne says.

It's like she read my mind. I was contemplating turning off the TV and pretending not to be home. Trouble would be my mom and Tyler. Neither are good at covert. But Jayne's right. I need to face this head-on.

I smooth my hand down my T-shirt. "I'll meet him outside."

"Atta girl," Jayne says.

"Who?" Mom says.

"I'm hanging up now," I tell Jayne and hold a finger up to tell Mom she's next.

"Good luck," Jayne says and disconnects.

"Someone's coming from Jayne's shop. I'm going to meet them outside. You good to hang with Tyler for a few minutes?"

"Sure," she says and gives me the once over. "You aren't meeting this person dressed like that?"

I cross my arms in defiance, about to claim I was, when I realize I'm not wearing a bra. "After I put on a bra," I say, and scuttle to my room. Being a Florida girl, I don't need to worry about shoes. We're used to walking on scorching sand, so a driveway is nothing.

"And maybe a better shirt," Mom calls behind me.

I'm outside in under five minutes. My van is in the driveway next to my mom's Nissan SUV. I pop the back and pull out the blankets from last night, balling them up and throwing them against my non-working garage door as a reminder to wash them. They're not grody or anything, but my mom brain demands I wash them anyway.

My house is cute. Built during the second world war, it's four blocks from the beach and just under fifteen hundred square feet. The bedrooms are so small a king size bed takes up the entire space. There's no such thing as a master suite.

The outside is white stucco with navy blue shutters. The roof is orange Spanish terra-cotta tiles, though many have turned black with age. I have two lovely palm trees in my yard that are probably as old as the house, if not older. They've weathered many hurricanes. I can't say as much for the roof tiles.

I sit in the back of my minivan and swing my legs back

and forth until a motorcycle creeps down my street and turns into my drive.

Dax pulls to a stop a few feet from me and swings his long leg over the bike before lifting off his helmet.

"Do you sit outside in your van often?" He smiles big and friendly.

"What are you doing here?" I can't afford friendly. The point of having a one night stand is to leave it at the *one night.* "I thought we agreed to let it be."

CHAPTER 8

SATURDAY

DAX GIVES A ONE SHOULDER SHRUG AND RUNS HIS HANDS through his hair. "We didn't say that specifically." He's dressed in jeans, heavy boots for riding, a flannel shirt with the sleeves rolled up, and a T-shirt underneath. "Besides, you promised you'd text to tell me you were okay, and when you didn't, I worried. How's your hip?"

He looks good enough to eat. I harden my resolve.

"Fine, just an ugly bruise. Dax, we were together until two. I figured you'd assume I was okay. *And* what we said, specifically, was that last night was good. Real good, and we agreed to leave it at a one-night stand."

He gives me a dazzling smile. "I didn't think you were serious about all that."

He's picked up some skills since we parted ways. Like the charming player-like smile. He can try his newfound moves on me, but they won't work.

I make myself swear not to give in. I stay on topic. "How did you find me, by the way?" I know how he found my house. But how did he find the boutique? I hadn't given him the name or any other detail.

"I did an internet search. Then narrowed it down from there. On the *Daily Mirror's* website is a picture of your friend Jayne, who was at the restaurant last night. I dug around the site and saw an email for you as well." He snapped his fingers. "Took seven minutes."

I'll be honest. Sarcasm is my default. It's how I set limits. And now was the time to use it on Dax. "Wow, you have a mechanical engineering degree, only because I helped you with the English assignments, but that's neither here nor there. You played in the NFL *and* you're a citizen sleuth. You. Are. The. Complete. Package."

He turns to rest against the seat of his bike. "I'm getting the vibe that I'm not wanted here." He gestures to my neighborhood. "Here being your beachfront house."

I point up the road. "Four blocks that way is the beach. I can hear the waves crashing from here." As if on a cue, a seagull squawks. Bless his scavenger heart.

"Loosely playing with the word 'beachfront,' though. Not that I care."

I make like I'm raining money, swiping one hand over my palm repeatedly. "Not all of us made fat cash right after college."

Dax puts his hands up in surrender. "Heather, I just came here because I wanted to say I really enjoyed last night. I'm in town for the next nine days for Bike Week, and I thought maybe we could see each other again. But it's clear you don't feel the same way."

Okay, so I feel a tad guilty for being bitchy. "It's just that you're on vacation, and this is my life. It's not like we're both in Hawaii and can leave it all behind when we get on a plane to go home."

"But we're not strangers," he says.

"We kinda are. We've had very different lives since college. I'm not Heather Lowell anymore. I'm Heather Michaels. I'm a single mom."

He nods as he considers my words. Then looks at me from under his brow. "I'd like to get to know Heather Michaels."

I shake my head. "For a week, and then you'll leave and go back to your real life. We should leave it at a one-night stand."

He puts one palm up. "How about a two-night stand?"

Against my better judgement, I laugh. "They don't exist."

"They should. So should three-night stands and four-night."

"That's called dating. Or a relationship."

"And you have no room for that?"

I shake my head. "Not right now. And what about you? I heard on talk radio you're being courted by a handful of NFL teams who want to add you to their coaching staff. Do you even know where you'll land when this is over?" I point to his bike.

He sighs and shifts his weight. "Well, hell, Heather, I can see your point. I'll be honest. This isn't how I saw this morning going."

I smile while telling myself I'm doing the right thing.

He picks up his helmet. "I guess I should get going. You all doing that restaurant thing tonight?"

I shake my head.

He plays with the strap. "You sure I can't convince you to go to dinner with me tonight at the very least?"

I hold firm to my resolve. "We had a no-strings-attached night, Dax. Isn't that what every guy wants? I truly don't expect anything more from you."

He blows out a sigh. "Okay." He meets my gaze.

Yeah, I'm sad he's going to leave and that'll be the last of him. But it truly is for the best. And the sooner he leaves, the sooner I can start looking for a lawyer and get to the bottom of expunging my record.

Behind me, the front door opens. I know this because the hinges need to be oiled and have a distinctive creak.

"Oh, my word. Is that you, Dax Griffin?" my mother calls from the front of the house.

Dax smiles and lifts a hand. "How are you, Mrs. Lowell?"

Mom comes outside and crosses the yard to Dax. "It's so good to see you. I watched you get that second concussion against that other California team and, Lord, it scared me. I wanted to email your momma because I knew she must be worried something fierce." She holds out her arms for a hug. Dax complies.

"Yeah," he says when they're done hugging. "She didn't like it much. She's part of the reason I left early. Kept showing me facts about concussions and brain integrity."

"As any good momma would do." She pats his cheek. Then gives a start as if she's struck by the best idea ever. "Dax, weren't you real good with fixing things? Mechanical things like dishwashers?"

"No, Mom." I leap out of the back of my van and rush toward them. "I said I'd take care of it."

She rolls her eyes. "Heather's dishwasher is broken. She won't let me buy her a new one." Mom's got her sing-song happy voice going. "But if you're still good with things like that and can tell me what parts to get, I'll go get them. She's busy enough with finishing college and raising Tyler, seeing to his medical needs, and with Justin always delinquent with child support...." She gives me a sidelong look. "You thought I didn't know about that, but I do. And when I see his momma I'm gonna give her an earful about her deadbeat son."

I slap my hand over my face. Heat from embarrassment rushes up my neck and flushes my face. I groan, "Mom."

"What?" She smacks her hand against her thigh. "It's not a sin to ask people for help. And you need help."

"I don't need help. I told you I'd take care of it." I dare not look at Dax, too mortified.

"So, Dax, care to give it a look?" Mom sings. She's like a dog with a bone. This is how she cons people. Like a siren with a song. Only she's a mom siren, and the lure is guilt.

"Sure. I still love to take things apart. Take me to this misbehaving dishwasher." He sets his helmet on his bike seat, gives me a sassy smirk, then follows my mom into my house.

I really want to kick over his bike. Then maybe kick my mom's SUV, too.

I didn't want Dax to know where I live.

I don't want Dax to know about my life.

And I certainly don't want him in my house.

Tyler comes running out, his eyes huge. "Momma, did you see who Mimi brought in the house? Dax Griffin. He used to play for—"

"Yes, I know. Remember how I told you that a long time ago your mom and Dax were friends? He popped by to say hi, and Mimi convinced him to take a look at the dishwasher."

Tyler loves football. He doesn't fully understand the

game, but something about it appeals to him. Lord knows, I've tried to figure out what. Maybe it's because they play rough, and he can't? Or maybe it's because he used to watch it with his dad, and that's how he keeps the bond. Tyler knows about Dax because the local sportscasters always talk about the local guys who made it big. That, and the fact that I went to college with Dax impresses Ty.

"Do you think he'll give me his writing?" He makes like he's scribbling.

Sometimes Tyler has a hard time finding the right words. Or even understanding what's being said. It's called a language processing disorder. What the doctors can't tell me is whether this processing disorder happened because of the seizures or alongside them. "His autograph? Yeah, I'm sure he will."

Tyler beams. "I'm gonna go watch."

"You stay out of his way," I say, but Tyler's already back in the house.

With a last look of longing toward the road as an escape from this mess, I head back inside.

Dax has stripped off his flannel shirt and pulled out the dishwasher. Mom is laying out the machine's ailments.

"And you cleaned out the trap?" he asks me.

I slap myself upside the head. "Duh, why didn't I think of that? You are so smart, Dax. Thanks for fixing the problem." I pick up his shirt and thrust it toward him. "Have a good day."

"Okay, I get it. You cleaned the trap. I had to ask." He starts the dishwasher.

"It's just going to fill up and not drain or run. Then when you open the door it will magically clean my kitchen floor." I reach across him and turn the dishwasher off. "I don't feel like mopping."

"It could be one of three things. The float switch isn't telling the machine when to shut off, the timer might be stuck, which again doesn't tell the machine to stop filling—"

"Or the inlet valve itself is stuck. I know. I researched it. But the YouTube videos on how to fix it are more than I can take on right now." I cross my arms, making my displeasure known.

"And a handyman costs too much," Tyler adds. "My medicine is more important, and that's where we put the money."

I hate that he's heard me say this. I rush to him, wrap him in a silly hug, and rock him back and forth while lifting him off the ground. He loves this. "That's because you can grow up to be my dishwasher so I'm investing in you. And your medicine is more important than a machine to do our dishes. You are what's most important. We don't need no stinking dishwasher. We have hugs." I squeeze him tighter, and he squeals.

I pepper him with kisses, and in between them say in a baby voice, "Mommy loves you."

Tyler simultaneously loves and hates this. He loved it as a smaller kid, but as he gets older, he says it's too babyish. But there's no mistaking the hug he gives me back.

"Stop, Momma. I'm not a baby." He's grinning.

I let him go just as quickly as I scooped him up. I pretend to wipe a tear. "You'll always be my baby."

He presses his forehead into my side, a sign of affection. "Can I help Dax fix the dishwasher?"

I meet Dax's eyes over Tyler's head. He gives a nod.

He says, "Dude, I totally need help. We need tools. You have those around here?"

Tyler rolls his eyes. "Yeah, but they're Mom's and they're pink."

Dax says, "Pink tools are still tools."

Tyler rushes out of the room to get the tools.

My mom says, "I'll go to the store and get the parts."

I groan. "No need. I bought them a while ago when I thought I might try to fix it myself." I reach under the kitchen sink and pull out some boxes from the back. "You have everything for any of the scenarios I thought it might be." My plan for buying all the options was to take back what I didn't need. Then time got away from me, and now I have a box of money spent that I could have saved.

Dax and my mom award me with big smiles. Like they've won or something.

"I'm going to take a shower," I say. I consider making a break for it by going out the bathroom window.

I lean close to Dax and say, "After this, you can't come back. Get on your bike and ride into the sunset."

He pats me on the shoulder. "You can thank me later."

CHAPTER 9
SATURDAY

MY MOTHER IS GONE, PLEASED TO LEAVE ME IN GOOD HANDS. Her words. Not mine. She was kinda right. Not only did Dax fix the dishwasher, but he also oiled the front door hinges and had lunch delivered to the house. Good food, too. Italian. A luxury I rarely allow myself. My kid loves it as well, so telling Dax no when Tyler was so excited to do something as extravagant as getting food delivered to the house would have made me the evilest mommy in all the land.

"Tyler." Dax pushes back slightly from the kitchen table. He rubs his belly as if to say he's stuffed. [

Tyler imitates him. "I'm gonna guess that you're a football fan."

I laugh. "What gives you that idea? Is it the football-themed jammies he had on earlier, the footballs all over this room and the house, or the incessant questions he's been asking you since you've been here?" I wink at Ty.

Dax clasps his hands behind his head and leans back. Tyler does the same.

Dax says, "None of the above. It was his knowledge about the game." He faces Tyler. "Talking football with you is like talking to one of the guys on my team. You know your stuff, kiddo. You gonna play?"

Tyler's hands drop to his lap, and he casts me a look filled with sadness. "No, Mom won't let me."

Dax, looking shocked, says, "What? Why?"

I don't want to go into my reasons because they're none of Dax's business. So instead, I shrug. "I have my reasons."

Tyler grunts with dissatisfaction. "It's because she's afraid I'll have a seizure."

Understanding crosses Dax's face. "That's what you need medicine for?" He cuts his eyes to me, and I nod.

How silly of me to think a kid could hold back information. Kids are, if nothing else, honest by default.

I say to Tyler, "It's not that I think football will *cause* a seizure. We've had this talk before. What if you have a seizure on the field while people are rushing after you? Or you're trying to catch the ball? And what about the collisions? Ask Dax here why he doesn't play anymore. It's because he's taken too many hits to the brain."

Tyler bows his head sadly. "And my brain already has problems."

How do you tell your kid that epilepsy is okay? Or that being smart enough to know you're slower than the other kids but don't know why is okay, too? I drop to the floor next to Tyler's chair and pull him around to face me.

"There is so much that you can do. You're smart and funny, and like Dax said, you know your football. Look at him, he's not even playing anymore. But he can use his football knowledge to do so many other jobs in the football field. He can coach or run a team, or with such a pretty face, he can be a sportscaster. Now they use computer guys to run analytics even. And you have those options, too. Remember, we talked about that? And there are people who help rehab the injured players. There are so many jobs in the field of football. And you can do any of them."

"Except play." His eyes are moist.

Oh, my heart, this kid. Am I being worked over a little? Yep. But I have to give him credit, he's persistent. And I know where this conversation is going. He wants to play flag football. Tyler may have epilepsy and a processing disorder, but he's clever. This little scene, while he's sad about not being able to play contact football, is about getting to play any type of football. He's been working me for a while now.

I say, "Maybe we can look into the flag football team."

His face lights up like I just handed him the keys to Disney World. "Really?"

"We can talk to Uncle Doug and the coach and see what they say." I make a silent prayer that the league rules wouldn't automatically exclude Tyler because of his medical condition.

Dax slaps his hand on one knee. "Well, if that's the case, we should go out in the yard and practice some plays."

Tyler leaps up. "Seriously? I'll go get my shoes." He dashes from the room.

Still squatting on the floor, I say, "Shouldn't you be leaving?"

He shakes his head. "No way. I like it here."

I roll my eyes. "But you have no reason to be here."

He gestures to the surrounding space. "I've helped with fixing stuff, and now I get to play with your kid. I think that's reason enough. It's not like I'm a burden."

I stand to stare at him, crossing my arms over my chest. "Why are you here, Dax? What do you want?"

He looks around the room then meets my stare. "This. I want this. I want to just chill and hang out. Yeah, I could hang out with the boys from the team and get rowdy. I could talk about the good old days, which were just a few months ago, oddly enough. I could do a million other things, but none of them are things I want to do. I want to relax. I want to play a little toss in the yard and not have anything or anyone pressing me to do more or be better."

He seems a little sad, and my resolve cracks. "And hanging with the guys causes you a lot of pressure?"

He gives an incredulous grunt. "Are you kidding? Those guys are trouble magnets, and it's like I'm the only adult. Keeping those guys out of trouble is a full-time job. Coming with them was stupid. I don't want to be a babysitter for grown men."

Tyler's closet door bangs as it slams against the wall. Like he slid it open in his haste to dress and find a football. Dax playing toss in the yard with him will be a memory Tyler will have forever. Another large crack in my resolve is created. I glance over my shoulder in the direction of Tyler's room.

Dax says, "He's a good kid."

I glance at Dax. "The best."

"Can I ask a personal question?"

"If I say no, will you not ask it?"

He ducks his head. "Nah, I'd just wait and ask it another time."

This I knew, because I knew Dax. He's nothing if not persistent. And patient. And even though we've gone several years without contact, he's still the same Dax.

"Ask then. Let's get it over with." I sit in my chair.

"How often does he see his dad?"

"Not very. Tyler had a bad seizure. Well, no seizure is good, but this was a big one. A grand mal. Usually I'm the one that handles those, but Tyler was at his dad's house when it happened. Justin didn't know what to do. He freaked out. I think it made him feel helpless. After that, he started missing his weekends. Always with an excuse, like work or something."

Dax sits in thought a moment. "Why do you make excuses for him?"

"For Justin?"

Dax nods. "Don't Tyler's seizures freak you out?"

I give a bitter smile. "Every time. I used to sit in the bathroom and cry afterward. But I'm getting better at not doing that." I don't want to say I was getting used to the seizures because I never will get used to that.

"If I was Tyler's dad, I'd find a way to learn how to handle my kid's seizures, and fast. It wouldn't cost me time with my kid."

And therein lies the difference between Justin and Dax. "Justin wasn't the best father before the seizures started, to be honest."

"If you'll let me, I'd like to spend the day with your kid. Play a little ball. You got a Madden or anything sports like? A gaming device?"

I hold my arms out, gesturing to my kitchen. "Do I look like I have the budget for a gaming device?" I hadn't meant to disclose my financial issues, but the conversation was so honest that I'd forgotten to keep my guard up with him. "Tyler plays Minecraft on his Kindle Fire."

Dax inspects me, though not in the obvious derisive way a person inspects someone he thinks isn't worthy. This is more like he's seeing me, Heather the mom, instead of Heather the college girl who used to lick whipped cream off of him.

"You're pretty amazing," he says.

"I already said you can stay and play ball with Tyler. You don't have to butter me up."

"Yeah, but you're letting me stay because you love him, not because you like my company." He smiles.

I give a one-shoulder shrug. "Might be true. You're leaving afterward, right?"

It's his turn to give a one-shoulder shrug. "Maybe. But afterward, Tyler and I might need to watch some football, or maybe we'll have to go out to dinner. Then there are football movies to watch."

I roll my eyes. This is not how I planned on spending my Saturday.

With that thought, the alarming realization that I was supposed to be investigating lawyers and ways to get my record expunged but hadn't sends a panic through me. A quick glance at the clock says I have a few hours left and I cross my fingers that Josie will have good news for me. If not, I hope some law offices work late on Saturdays.

I stand quickly. "Okay, well make sure he doesn't get too overheated. If his face gets flushed, you need to take a break. I need to make a few phone calls. I'll be in my room." I point down the hallway. "If you're going to explain things, don't be too wordy. He can only process small chunks at a time." I give him a thumbs up. "Got it?"

He smiles. "Got it. Are you sure we'll be okay together?" he teases.

I point to the smartwatch on my wrist. "Tyler is wearing a watch similar to this. If he has a seizure, I'll be alerted. Probably before you even realize it."

"So, it's *not* that you fully trust me. I get it. Go do your thing." He waves me off.

I hesitate for only a second. Yeah, Dax's *got it*. But how would he be in a real-time event? Hopefully, we won't find out. Hopefully, Tyler will have a blast and be left with nothing but wonderful memories.

With the guys outside, I call Josie. She tells me she's connected with a prominent lawyer known to handle these cases and will do so in a timely manner. After Josie's review of my record, she thinks getting it expunged will be easy. The real obstacle tis time. She's waiting to hear back from the other lawyer with an estimate.

We disconnect, me still in limbo. I sit at the small built-in desk in my kitchen and use my laptop to search out other degree options, but don't come away with anything of interest that's not going to require several more years in school.

Feeling a little hopeless as the clock quickly ticks down to my deadline, I go into the living room where Dax and Tyler are playing Battleship.

Dax is tempting us both with going out to eat when he gets a phone call. He steps outside to take it, briefly glancing at me through the sliding door. When he comes back in, he's distracted.

"Listen, I'm sorry, but there's something I have to take care of. Can I get a raincheck and do dinner out another night?"

Tyler's face is crestfallen.

I stroke my son's head. "Sure, Dax."

Less than ten minutes later, he's out the door. I'm grateful I kept my expectations to zero. And this sadness that he's gone is only because he made the day different, and different is always refreshing and hard to let go. Right? Of course, that's it.

CHAPTER 10

MONDAY

JAYNE PAUSES, BOX CUTTER IN HAND, AND SAYS, "SO YOU'RE telling me you had great sex in the back of your minivan, he shows up the next day—"

"No thanks to you," I remind her.

"Right. I buggered that up. Sorry again. But it sounds like I did you a favor."

"Yeah," Josie says. "He fixed your dishwasher and gave your kid a day he'll remember forever."

The three of us are in the back room of Jayne's shop, The Daily Mirror, unboxing her latest fashion finds from her most recent European trip. Jayne's boutique specializes in unique and personalized style for the everyday girl, but also high-end haute couture for clients she acts as a personal shopper for. Local elites who like to get clothing pieces no others in town have while pretending they're doing the local economy a favor by supporting Jayne's small business.

Only, her shop's not so small anymore. A few years ago, she thought about opening a second shop but ended up taking The Daily Mirror online with a personal shopping and outfit matching service called The Daily Closet. After customers upload a picture of themselves, Jayne and her two apprentices help them choose outfits and accessories for all occasions. Jayne makes money hand over fist, something her momma loved to say.

I say, "Yes, he did fix my dishwasher and really made Tyler happy playing ball. At bedtime, Ty kept saying no kid his age gets to play catch with a pro football player."

Josie sits on a worktable and swings her legs while she eats an apple. Her long black hair is done in an Elsa braid that makes her look like a fairy princess. Well, a fairy princess with really big boobs and henna all over her body.

She says, "Then Dax just left?"

I shrug because Dax's parting was the darnedest thing. And how I felt about it was more frustrating because I didn't want him at my house in the first place, but when he left, I wanted him to stay.

I say, "He got a phone call as we were talking about going out for dinner. I had tacos on the menu, but Dax insisted on treating us. Then his phone rang, he took the call outside, and when he came in, he apologized, spent a few more minutes with Ty, and then he left."

From a box on the table, Jayne takes out an Italian leather purse that cost what I make in a week. "And you didn't see him Sunday?"

I shake my head. And I was mad at myself for checking out the front window every time I walked by while cleaning the house. My dishwasher ran like a champ, and I wanted to thank him again. Not doing dishes by hand is a luxury.

Josie chucks the apple core across the room at the trash can. It hits the rim and bounces in.

"Lucky," Jayne says.

"All skill," Josie says before she turns her attention to me. "Do you want anything from Dax, Heather? Like maybe even a relationship?"

"Nope," I say, more from habit than actual heart.

She says, "Would you sleep with him again?"

I'd sure thought about it a lot since he left. "That would be stupid."

Jayne's brows shoot up. "That wasn't a no."

Josie chuckles. "Because memories of it are keeping her awake at night."

We ignore her. Of all our friends, she's the most courageous, overt, and sexual.

Jayne says, "My guess is, the reason he left like he did was because of whoever called."

"And you're sure he doesn't have a wife," Josie says. As a divorce lawyer, she's also the most cynical.

"I've never seen an announcement and his social media says he's single. But it's not like social media always tells the truth." I say. But doubt is there. It never left, really.

"Maybe a girlfriend?" Again Josie.

Jayne tosses a roll of packing tape at Josie. "Why are you telling her this guy is a wanker? What if he's a right bloke?"

Josie shrugs and gives me an apologetic smile. "I think everyone should go in knowing the downside, is all. I bet he's a good guy and maybe the phone call was an emergency."

I shake my head. "He would have said something about that." I swipe my hand across the space in front of me. "Never mind. It's over. He's gone, and I got what I wanted."

Jayne wags her brows and says with an exaggerated English accent, "Yer boots knocked."

Time for a subject change. "I have bigger problems, anyway. Josie heard back from the lawyer. He said the courts are backed up, and an expedited expunging will take a minimum of three months. I shared that news with my counselor, so I'm officially *not* on the list for a student teaching position this fall."

Josie stops swinging her legs. "I'm so sorry. I wish I could have turned it around faster. Have you made a decision about graduation?"

I shake my head and choke back tears. "You know what bugs me? Even if I get my record expunged, I still have to disclose it on job applications." This was a fun fact Josie shared with me yesterday as well. "Jamison said I have to decide soon. Class registration is next week, and we need a plan."

Jayne asks, "Is there another degree you might want to pursue instead? Something else you might like to do?"

My throat gets clogged with emotion, and a tear trickles down one cheek. "I wanted this," I say hoarsely.

Jayne moves next to me and throws her arms around my shoulders in a side hug. "I know you did. Until you get this thing worked out, you'll always have a job here. Don't let that be a stressor."

Josie says, "We started the paperwork anyway. Brinn said he'd donate to a campaign if we thought it would help."

"How much do I owe you?"

She waves me off.

I push away from Jayne and toss my box cutter on the table. "Stop. Y'all can't keep rescuing me*]*. My parents buy me tires, Jayne gives me a job, Dax fixes my dishwasher, Josie gives me a huge discount on my divorce, Paisley gives me her furniture after she moved in with Hank when she could have sold it. I can't continue to be a charity case."

Josie huffs. "I think you're confusing family, friendship, and love with charity."

"I want to do this on my own," I say.

Jayne looks confused. "Why, when you have people around you who want to help? Only those who have no one are forced to do it alone. Sadly. And when given a choice to have support or not, why would you choose not to?"

I slump against the back wall and duck my head into my hands. Through my fingers, I say, "I just need to prove to myself I can do it."

Josie says, "And the fact that you've been doing it every day alone for the last what...three years, isn't proof enough?"

I look up at her. "Says the woman who walked away from her cushy life and law degree to find her brother. How many odd jobs did you work? And how much help did you take from your family? None, right?"

She leans against the wall with me. "Yes, I see your point. I did turn my back on my family. But strangers helped me along the way]. That's how I got some of those odd jobs. When my car broke down on the side of the road when I was moving here, I took a ride from two unknown guys. I took help."

Jayne smiles. "The fact that she ended up marrying one of those guys who gave her a ride is an oddity. None of us are asking you to join us in wedded bliss or the shacking up equivalent."

Josie nudges me with her shoulder. "All that to say, we're here if you need us. Jayne's come this far in her company because you helped her run this business while she started the online portion. I think we keep going on about it because we're afraid you won't ask. Hell, I'd do your expunging for free, but I know you won't let me."

I did feel a little foolish, digging in my heels. Yet, I needed to prove to myself I was capable. I reach out and take Josie's hand. "I promise to ask for help and not let pride win."

She smiles. "That's all we want."

We do a group hug. I'm very thankful for these women. I want them to know that.

"I'm lucky to have you all," I say.

"I feel the same," says Josie. Jayne echoes her.

My phone alarm jingles, jolting us from our reverie.

"How could I forget?" I say. "That's my reminder for my appointment with Tyler's neurologist."

Thankfully, I set reminders two hours out. I have a forty-minute drive to north Orlando for the appointment. It's a meeting to go over his current medication and sleep study results. Thankfully, Tyler doesn't have to endure it.

The drive is quick; I mostly do it on autopilot. I sign in at the front desk and make one wish for the day, that the news is better than good. Then I think of Dax, wondering if he makes wishes regularly like I do.

I take a seat next to a woman who looks like a deer caught in headlights. I know that look. I've had it several times. It's fear. Fear of what the doctor will say. Fear of how you'll handle it. Fear of the billion unknowns that you can't even begin to wrap your mind around. Will my child be okay? Will he have a good life? How can I bear as much of his burden as possible for them him?

She stares at the clipboard, her pen hovering over the page. But not moving. Only blinking. She's dressed well, makeup done, hair styled. But she's missed a button on her shirt, and her nails looked chewed from worry. I used to look like her when Tyler's seizures were new and I thought, if I kept life the same, they'd disappear as suddenly as they'd come. But like this woman next to me, I was falling apart inside, and it was creeping its way out.

I touch her arm, and she jumps.

"First time, right?" I say quietly.

She nods. Tears puddle in her eyes. I don't say it's going to be okay because I don't know. We never do.

"You can do this," I say. "It's okay to be scared. There's so much to take in. Just go one step at a time."

"How old?" She gulps. "How old is your child?"

"Eight next month, but he was diagnosed at four. Yours?"

"Four. She's just a baby." The tears spill down her face.

"I know. And it's so unfair. What's her name?"

"Madison."

I take the clipboard from her then write Madison on the form. "What's your name?"

"Lisa. Lisa Foster."

I stick out my hand. "Hi, Lisa Foster. I'm Heather Michaels." We shake, and I squeeze her hand softly to give her strength. Then I write her name on the correct line on the form. "Can I help you with this?" I tap my pen to the paper.

She nods.

We fill out the form together. Me acting as scribe. She tells me about Madison, and I tell her about Tyler. I invite her to the Facebook support group I run for parents of kids with learning difficulties and epilepsy. She joins on the spot.

"Doctor Carpenter is amazing. She'll say a lot today, but everything she tells you she'll have on paper for you to read later because you won't remember everything from this appointment. But you can reach out to me if you need to go over it again afterward or have any questions. I can try to help."

Lisa nods.

I give her a side hug. We're from the same tribe. It's the our-kids-have-a-diagnosis-and-we're-scared tribe.

Doctor Carpenter is standing in the doorway that separates the waiting room from the back offices. She smiles at me. "Heather, you ready, or do you need a few minutes?"

I ask Lisa if she's okay. She nods. Following another hand squeeze, I leave her behind to follow the good doctor and wait for the news she has to share. Good or bad.

We take a seat in her office, and she smiles. "That was something out there. What you did for her."

I shrug. "Mom helping a mom."

"Not a lot of people are good at that. Working with scared parents."

"Maybe because I've been there it's easier?"

She studies me for a second. "I have a personal question, and I apologize for being so nosy, but did you go to college?"

I blow out a sigh. "I'm almost done. I have a minor in psychology and I'm looking at getting my bachelors in child studies." This is what Jamison called the new track she wants to put me on.

Doctor Carpenter's smile gets large. "Heather, I have an opportunity you might be interested in."

CHAPTER 11

MONDAY

I TEXT MY FRIENDS AFTER LEAVING DR. CARPENTER'S. WOW, what an appointment it was. Marvelous news about Tyler's sleep study and medication. Stable and long periods of no seizure activity is just what I like to hear. Her offer was the cherry on top.

On the drive home I fill in my counselor, Jamison, having caught her right before she left the office. Then I fill Mom in on Tyler's results when I pick him up from my mom's.

I ask the gang to meet me at my house, and I splurge. I grab takeout Thai food for everyone. I only balked once at the cost. But I don't care. I'm celebrating that maybe, just maybe, my luck has turned.

We get home ten minutes before my friends arrive. Josie's carrying wine. Paisley has cookies. It's officially a girls' night.

Paisley says, "I'm glad you called when you did before I made the drive home to Jacksonville. I'm finding once I get on the road, I don't want to turn back."

Last month Paisley moved in with Hank, who's stationed in Jacksonville. Her daily commute is an hour and a half one way, but she only has ten more weeks of the school year left before she's done for good. Paisley, an occupational therapist like my sister-in-law Kenley, will be saying goodbye to her school therapy job, getting married, and moving to Japan.

I forgot about her commute. "I'm sorry," I say. "I appreciate you coming, but you don't have to stay if you want to get on the road."

She flings an arm around my shoulder. "Are you kidding? I won't miss that traffic for nothing. Besides, Hank has duty, so he's sleeping on base, and I can stay with Josie. It's a win for everyone. And I smell Thai food, so there's no way you're getting rid of me now."

I'll miss her desperately. It was Paisley who'd been the kind, gentle person to guide me down Tyler's medical path. She's been my unwavering light in the storm. I side-hug her back.

"I can't stand it," Jayne says. "Tell us the news!"

They're gathered in my kitchen. Tyler's already dug through the many boxes of food and taken what he wants. He's disappeared into the living room to watch TV.

"Okay, get this," I say and clasp my hands together in excitement. "Tyler's seizures haven't increased and the medicine seems to be keeping him stable."

The group cheers, and Jayne hugs me while jumping up and down.

Josie holds up a wine bottle in each hand. "I should have brought champagne, not red wine."

I wave my hands to get their attention. "Wait, that's not all. Though by far that's the best news, but get this." I tell them about how I helped Lisa fill out her forms in the doctor's waiting room. That I used the same calm, soft mannerisms Paisley did with me. I tell them how Dr. Carpenter witnessed it. "And... she offered me a job."

The group gasps in delight.

"A job?" asks Jayne. "What sort?"

I take plates out of the cabinet and hand one to each of them. "It's called a child life specialist. It's working with families and kids as they go through these big life events. Surgeries, the unthinkable, you name it."

Paisley pauses as she's scooping rice. "That's actually perfect for you. I wish I'd thought of it." She meets my gaze. "It's not always going to be an easy job. But then, neither is teaching."

Josie asks, "And you can do this with your criminal record?" She winks.

I smile. "Yes, I still want to get the record expunged, but it's not essential. I told Dr. Carpenter about it and she didn't seem worried. I already spoke with my college counselor and I have most of the required classes. I'm two short, but I can take them as online evening classes. So that's good. What's even better is that I can graduate at the end of summer if I want."

Paisley asks, "Isn't there an internship? If I remember right, when I was doing mine, there was another gal there doing one as a child life specialist."

This was the downside to this new opportunity. Though, in perspective, it was really no different from my student teaching. "Yes, I'll have to do a three-month internship starting in May at the hospital in Orlando, which is where the position will be." Not the logistically perfect internship of working in Tyler's school, as I'd hoped. The drive alone would be a juggle. Previously, I had planned to work after school at Jayne's shop until six-thirty, giving me fifteen hours a week, but now that extra time would be eaten up by my drive to and from Orlando. I'd planned for the cut in pay a year ago by saving what I could. But now I'll be even shorter on income than expected because, not only would I start sooner than expected, but the additional loss of income is a hard hit for a hand-to-mouth household. [My friends know this. We've drafted loads of budgets trying to plan for the worst-case scenario.

Josie asks, "Is it paid?"

I make the 'sorta' sign with my hand. "There's a stipend to cover gas and meals."

There's an unanswered question hanging heavy in the room. Can I afford to take this opportunity? For me, the answer is: how could I not? This career sounds every bit as good as teaching. It's helping others in ways I never imagined. And my "criminal record" is a non-issue.

I try to work out the logistics and talk through the issues with my friends. "Childcare is taken care of with my mom."

Paisley adds, "Your increase in gas will be covered, too. That's good. And maybe you can pocket the difference by taking your own lunches."

I say, "Which I would do anyway."

Jayne is tapping her finger to her lip. She stops and says, "I can find you work. There's always inventory and uploading pictures and stuff. Some of which you can do from home. You tell me what hours you want to work, and I'll make it happen."

I want to weep at her generosity. "I don't know what I can commit to. Weekends maybe? It's only for three months, and Tyler and I can make adjustments in the short term for a long-term gain."

Paisley says, "We should start you a GoFundMe."

I groan. "Please don't."

"I'd contribute," Josie says.

"Me too," echoes Jayne.

I cover my ears. "I'm going to ignore you. You know how I feel about these things."

Josie, who'd been putting Pad Thai on her plate, stops and sets everything down before she faces me, hands on hips. "I hate to be the downer in the room, but if you're doing classes at night and working long hours in the day, you aren't going to have a lot of time to work for Jayne. Let us help. We can afford it."

"I did a quick re-figuring of my budget on the drive home. As I see it, I have a month and a half covered. Maybe I can take out another student loan to cover the difference? I'll find a solution," I say with more assurance than feel.

Josie opens her mouth to protest, I'm sure, when the doorbell ringing stops her.

"I'll get it," Paisley says. She hands me her plate. She comes back moments later leading Dax into the room. He's carrying a large plastic grocery bag. Tyler is at his heels, clearly thrilled to see him again.

Dax says, "You're having a party, and I didn't get invited. My feelings are hurt." He feigns a sad face.

"I deleted your number," I lie. But I'm peeved he left so suddenly on Saturday.

And darn him. He looks so good I can't help but take him in for a moment. I blame the wine. His dark green T-shirt stretches across his broad shoulders, and his jeans are snug across his muscular thighs. I bet if he turned around, his jeans would be cupping his bum in all the right places.

"You could've messaged me on Instagram, seeing as you follow me." He winks.

"Now I'm glad I didn't invite you," I say, and hand Paisley back her plate. I don't get one for Dax, but Jayne does.

"What's the occasion?" he asks.

The room is quiet. I suspect my friends are letting me give him only the information I want him to have.

But Tyler beats me to it. "Mom got a job but first she has to do something called an enter-ship. I don't know what that is. It sounds like it has something to do with aliens. And the job's in Orlando, so she'll be driving a lot. But Mom doesn't know how she's going to pay for everything while she's on the enter-ship. I guess that means I'll be staying with Mimi a lot. Because my dad is a deadbeat." He looks at me wide eyes. "I hope you come back from the enter-ship."

I brush a lock of hair from his forehead. "You have to stop saying your dad is a deadbeat."

"Uncle Doug said it when he tried to fix the dishwasher before Dax fixed it. He was telling Mimi it was too bad my dad was such a deadbeat and it pisses him off you have to worry about money."

I pull him close to me. "First, 'pisses' is a bad word. Please don't say it anymore. And second, that's Uncle Doug's opinion about your dad. It doesn't mean it's true. I don't think your dad is a deadbeat. Your dad gave me you. How could that make him bad? Never. It never could."

Tyler smiles and leans into me. "You won't get stuck on this ship, will you?"

"It's called an INTERN-ship. That means, while they train me and teach me the job, I work for free. Once I know everything, they start to pay me because then I don't need someone with me all the time to make sure I don't goof up."

His face brightens. "That's a relief."

I say, "You're telling me. I'm woefully unprepared to deal

with aliens, space travel, and anything that comes with that." The group chuckles.

"Can I have more noodles?" he says. I oblige and dump them on his plate. Afterward, he escapes back to the living room.

Dax says, "Wow, sounds like today was a great day." He puts his plate on the table. "Looks like I made a good call when I stopped by the store for this." He opens the grocery bag and takes out three gallons of various flavored ice cream and endless toppings including sprinkles and toffee. Both my favorite.

Josie claps Dax on the shoulder. "You can stay." She picks up a jar of maraschino cherries with the stems still on. "Why the stems?"

He grins. "Did you know Heather can tie knots in the stems. She once won two hundred dollars at a party doing it."

I laugh, having forgotten that night. "Maybe I could do that now to get some extra cash."

"I'd pay," Dax says as he loads his plate.

Is it just me, or can everyone feel the electricity arc between us? I hope not. But going by their goofy grins and winks, I'm guessing they do.

Instantly, my chest flares up with the heat of embarrassment.

Jayne to the rescue. "Okay, ladies. We can figure this out so our girl can make her new dream come true."

Paisley says. "But first, wine."

We all hold out our glasses for refills.

Then Dax kills the mood when he says, "I can just give you the money, Heather."

CHAPTER 12

MONDAY

Paisley shakes her head and then says to Josie and Jayne, "Let's get out of here. I want to be able to tell the police he was alive when we left."

Dax looks around the room confused. "What am I missing?"

My three friends look at me expectantly. I presume they think I'm going to erupt. Had today not been on the spectacular side, I might have already exploded. But today's been too good for me to want to ruin it with a fight.

Though I do have enough indignation on behalf of all the single moms out there to put some heat in my words. "Tell me Dax, do you just hand out large sums of money to random strangers? Women you think need it?"

He looks to my friends, probably hoping for a clue as to how to answer. Chicken. Then he returns his attention to me. "Not the way you put it, but yeah, I do. I'm involved in a few charities that help single parents."

"And I could tap into a charity like that if I wanted, couldn't I?"

He shrugs. "Sure, there's a process and you have to qualify. But you'd definitely qualify."

"If you handed me some dollars without me having to go through any process, it would be like jumping ahead in the line. Maybe cheating someone who needs it more than me."

"No, because me handing you the money doesn't affect how much I give to those organizations. They still get money from me. You would only be jumping ahead if I used their pot of money. But I'm not. You're my friend, so I'm offering you money from my wallet. That doesn't affect the charities I donate to."

A lifestyle I'm sure I'll never be familiar with. "Are you telling me you are so flushed with cash that you could afford to give to your charities and to me and not even blink?" It's not like I'm asking how much he has in savings, or anything.

He nods. "Yeah, I am. Not solely from my league pay, but from endorsement deals, too. Listen." He holds up a hand to stop me from continuing the argument. "I never meant to offend you. But life has been good to me. I like to pay it forward. If I can help you, that would mean even more to me than helping a person I get to know through reading an application submitted to the charity. Helping you would make me feel good. Would make me feel like the concussions were worth it."

His argument takes the steam right out of me. "Thing is, Dax. You giving me money wouldn't make me feel good. Whether right or wrong, I'd feel obligated. Like, if I were to splurge on a dress for me or takeout, you might resent that a little because those are luxuries I can't afford, yet I'm taking them from the money you'd be giving me."

"I wouldn't begrudge you those things."

I shrug. "Maybe you think you wouldn't. But I see it all the time. Heck, just go through social media, and you'll see it. A person who's got extra money and spends it after payday can do something like, I dunno, get a manicure to make themselves feel better. A person like me, who lives paycheck to paycheck, can't do that because then we're looked at as irresponsible. We're not allowed things that make us feel better until we pull ourselves out of the situation we're in. And I don't want to have that happen between us"—I face my friends—"or us."

Dax nods, his way of processing what I've said. Then he meets my gaze and says, "If I had one wish, it would be for that not to be true."

Something warm and pleasant courses through me. Maybe it's because I'm surrounded by people who genuinely care for me. But whatever it is, it fills my cup. "Me, too. Trust me, if it weren't true, all my problems would be solved," I joke. "Because I've got lots of people who want to give me money."

We laugh, my joke having broken the tension.

"Wow," Paisley says, "That went way different than I thought it would."

"Right," Jayne says. "I'm relieved he's not dead."

"Me, too," Dax says and makes like he's wiping sweat from his head.

We laugh, and I punch him in the arm.

Tyler walks into the room. "What's so funny?"

I ruffle his hair. "Nothing, adult humor."

He raises a lip. "I don't get adult humor."

Josie says, "You will one day. But for now, did you see what Dax brought?"

She shows him the ice cream and all the extras. His eyes go wide.

"Can I have more than one topping?" His look is pleading.

I smile. "Tonight is a celebration and, because you are almost eight, I will let you have eight toppings."

Tyler's face lights up.

Paisley picks up the ice cream scooper. "What flavor should I start with, Ty?"

We get Tyler set up with a large bowl of ice cream covered with a mixture of candies and syrup that I'm sure will make his stomach upset.

"Can I eat this in the living room? On TV is a Ninja Turtle marathon."

"Booyakasha," I say, and we pound fists.

He pauses before slipping into the living room. He points at Dax. "Don't leave without saying goodbye."

Dax holds up a hand like he's doing scouts honor. "I promise."

"What about us?" Josie calls to Tyler's backside as he scurries from the room.

"I see you all the time," Tyler grumbles.

Josie harrumphs then winks. "Well, we've been replaced by this one." She jerks her thumb to point to Dax.

"Message received, loud and clear," Jayne says. "Let's scoop some to-go dessert, and we'll let these two be alone."

Dax grabs a hot fudge jar. "Don't leave on my account." He goes to the microwave and opens it. No light comes on.

Dax points to it. "Does this work?"

"Yes," I say. "The bulb's burned out, but it works."

"Unlike your garage door," Paisley says then faces Dax.

"She doesn't park in her garage because the garage door opener jams all the time."

I say, "Oh, my Lord, Paisley. What is that about?"

She shrugs. "Josie said he fixed your dishwasher. I figured he might want to take a look at your garage door opener."

Josie holds up one finger. "Didn't you have a gutter problem, too?"

I cover my eyes in humiliation. Maybe when I uncover my eyes, my friends will be magically gone.

I let my hands fall. Nope, they're still in my kitchen and smiling at me.

The microwave chimes that Dax's fudge is done.

"See, it works," I say.

Josie pulls a spoon from the utensil drawer and hands it to him. "We'd like to get to know you better, Dax. Seeing as how Heather is one of our favorite people and we love her and will protect her."

Dax pauses, spoon halfway between the fudge and his ice cream bowl. "Message received."

Paisley smiles. "That's good. Because Josie has a stun gun and likes to use it."

Josie rolls her eyes. "We'll leave you to it and then we'll all grill you at a later date."

I cross my arms. "No reason to grill him. We're friends from college, and he's here for Bike Week. He's leaving when it's over, right?"

Dax shrugs. "Maybe. I don't have any plans. I'm between careers and currently trying to figure things out."

Josie claps him on the back. "Just use a condom if you happen to find yourself on our friend here."

"Get out," I say and point to the front of the house. I'm all talk. I know Josie means well, and I love her for it. Even if it is embarrassing.

My friends hug me goodbye as I see them out.

Afterward, Dax and I stand in my small foyer, the front door behind me, the entry to living room behind him. He wolfs down the remains of his ice cream, arching one brow as he spoons it into his mouth.

"Why are you here?" I ask.

He chews, swallows, then says, "Because this is where I want to be."

"The way you rushed out of here on Saturday makes me think what you just said isn't entirely true." I cross my arms and lean against the door.

He leans against the wall and kicks one foot over the other. "Something unexpected came up, and I had to handle it."

"Most people would say, 'Something's happened and I have to take care of it'."

He looks into the bowl, frowns, then shows me it is empty. "Yeah, I could have said that, but I know you. You would have thought I had a secret girlfriend or something real nefarious."

I squint at him, hoping to convey I think he's crazy. "Nefarious? Like you're running drugs or something. Don't be stupid." I roll my eyes. "And you're right. I do think you have a secret something-or-other that's going to show up here and make a scene. Because saying nothing left me to consider all the possibilities." I point to the living room. "I have a child in there who I will go down in flames to protect—"

He holds up a hand, a smile on his lips. "There's no secret anything that's gonna show up. I'd never put Tyler in any situation that could cause him physical or emotional harm. Never. Can I just say you're so sexy when you get all momma bear?"

I clear my throat. "We were talking about your sudden departure and why you're back again."

With a jerk of his head, he gestures for us to go back to the kitchen which, oddly, is more private. Once there, he rinses his bowl and puts it in the dishwasher. A task most women would find sexy because a man cleaning up after himself is a catch.

Dax says, "Okay, don't hate me, but I was thinking about our night in the van and I was thinking about how I did some things that weren't my best. I could do better. I thought maybe we could go at it again, and I could show you my good stuff."

"You're saying I didn't get the best that night?" I lean against the counter and cross my arms. This is gonna be fun.

He does the same. "I thought it was my best. But in hindsight, I think I might have been holding back. Afraid to overwhelm you. I think we should do it again so I can measure the two against each other."

Briefly, I press my lips together to keep from smiling. "Are you saying you want to measure my performance, too?" He walked right into that one.

He straightens. "No, you were outstanding. Actually, better than outstanding. It's me. I think I didn't do my best."

I make like I'm uncertain. "Problem is, we agreed to a one-night stand, and if we did it again, then... well... you know."

"Except it's a new week. A new line on the calendar. If we gave it another go, then we can call it this week's one night."

I pretend to consider his rebuttal. "So, theoretically, each week we could have a one-nighter."

He nods. "Downside to that is it limits us to once a week." He looks at me from under his brow.

Dang, he's so sexy and cute, wrapped up in a fun-loving, easygoing package. He spent the evening with my friends and didn't look pained once. He spends time with Tyler and appears to genuinely enjoy it.

And he finds me sexy. That alone is heady stuff. When my definition of self is worn out and haggard, it does something wonderful to my self-esteem to know a man I find attractive thinks my worn out and haggard is sexy.

"Okay," I say. "I'd like to know, too, if you can raise the bar."

His mouth goes slack. "Seriously, I thought for sure you'd say no and kick me out."

I point a finger at his face. "Tyler can't know."

He shakes his head. "Of course not."

"And it's one night."

He holds up one finger. "Got it. One."

He's not been good with 'one' so far.

"How long are you in town?" I ask him.

"The plan was to head to Tampa when Bike Week ends. Six more days."

"Perfect, that all falls on the calendar as this week. So, based on your argument about one one-night stand a week, we only have this one night left."

He snaps his fingers in disappointment. "Darn it, I should've thought that through better." But the smile teasing at his lips tells me a different story. He's not worried. Because he'll come up with another argument tomorrow, and I can't wait to hear it.

"Can I kiss you?" he says.

I nod.

He walks slowly toward me, like a puma stalking its prey. I'm backed up against the counter, and his hands go to my sides and box me in.

He lowers his head and swipes a kiss across my lips. Then another. By the third one, I'm meeting him halfway. It takes only three kisses to have me chasing him for more. I wrap my arms around him and pull him close. Time stops as I get lost in him, his kisses and the wonderful feelings that come with being held in his arms.

It's a make-out session reminiscent of high school, pelvises brushing each other, lots of kissing and nibbling. Only this time I have one ear for any sound of Tyler headed our way. Dax's hand toys with the hem of my shirt. Mine is gripping his hip bone, pulling him toward me. We're going too far, too fast, like an out-of-control rollercoaster ride and I have my hands up ready to give in]to the thrill.

I push him away. "I have to get Tyler to bed."

He backs up a step and swipes his hand down his face. Then blows out a slow breath. "I forgot where I was there for a moment."

I beam. To know you do something magical to the person who is doing something equally wonderful to you is a self-esteem boost of epic proportions.

I yell into the living room, "Time to shut it down, honey. It's bedtime."

"Aw, Mom," Tyler says, but the TV clicks off.

He comes into the kitchen moments later. "Are you leaving Dax?"

I say, "Not yet. Mom and Dax are going to hang out a bit."

Tyler points to Dax. "You promised you'd say bye."

Dax crosses his heart.

I rub chocolate off my son's face. "Bathroom. Brush your teeth. Take a wet towel to your face, too. Or I will. I'll tuck you in when you're done."

He groans but does as I ask.

Dax and I stand in the kitchen staring at each other. If he's as revved as me, he's probably counting the minutes until Ty falls asleep.

I put my fingers to my lips, "If we're going to do this we will have to be very quiet. Ty must not know."

He whispers, "Challenge accepted."

CHAPTER 13

TUESDAY MORNING

Last night, we sat outside and talked about everything and nothing while waiting for Tyler to go to bed. We reminisced about college, and Dax shared stories from the NFL that cracked me up. What we didn't talk about was his plans. Or anything beyond this week. We kept everything casual. No strings.

Then Tyler fell asleep, and it was game on. We were as quiet as church mice but as naughty as devils. And if I thought sex with Dax in my minivan was good, in my bed it was a spiritual experience. The sort that makes a person weak in the knees and a believer in out-of-this-world experiences. And yes, his game performance last night differed from the minivan tryst. Both were oh-so-very-good.

The banging of the bathroom door slamming wakes me.

With a start, I sit up, disoriented. The sun's bright and the birds are chirping and I'm stark naked.

Dax lies beside me softly snoring, also naked as a baby.

The toilet flushes, and my brain makes the connection. Tyler is up and about. A quick glance at my clock tells me I'd forgotten to set my alarm, and we are forty minutes behind schedule.

Usually, I'm the one who wakes Tyler. On weekends, when I manage to sleep in, he wakes me by barging into my room.

Bathroom first stop. My room next. I lunge at the door and flip the lock.

After putting on my robe, I go back to the bed and place my hand over Dax's mouth.

His eyes slam open.

"It's morning and Tyler's awake. You need to get out of here before he sees you."

He nods. I remove my hand. The doorknob jiggles.

"Mom, we slept in," Tyler says.

Dax is up and trying to get his pants on. I shove him into my closet with only one leg in his jeans. I toss the rest of his clothes and boots in behind him, catching him in the forehead with the sole of one boot.

He winces but stays quiet. I close the bifold closet doors as quietly as possible. Then go to my door and open it.

"We need to hurry. You're going to be late for school."

My son stares up at me wide-eyed. "Are you sick?"

He asks this because I never sleep in on work and school days. I shake my head and tighten the belt on my robe. Thankful I'd picked the hot pink robe over the light yellow, or I'd worry it was see-through.

"No, I think with all the excitement yesterday and the company, I stayed up later than usual. I went to bed too tired and forgot to set my alarm.

Tyler studies me. For an almost-eight-year-old, he's clever. Observant. Has to be when trying to always be one step ahead of everyone else because the information you get isn't always reliable. Such is the burden of kids with processing disorders.

"Can I have waffles for breakfast?"

These are a weekend treat.

"Yes, but heat them up. It's gross that you eat them frozen." We have this conversation a lot.

Tyler leans into my room and looks around, then looks at the closet and says, "Dax, you want some waffles? I can put them in the toaster for you."

My mouth falls open. "What makes you think Dax is here?"

Tyler's look is the equivalent of saying *DUH*. "Because he promised to say goodbye, and he didn't."

I have no response.

Tyler says to the closet, "Mom bought blueberry syrup, Dax. It's pretty good."

From behind the closed doors, Dax says, "No thanks, Buddy. But I appreciate the offer."

Tyler shrugs as if it's no big deal to him and turns, heading to the kitchen, never bothering to ask why Dax might be in the closet. Maybe to an almost-eight-year-old, this isn't weird.

I close the bedroom door before I open the closet door. Dax is leaning against the wall, my clothes crushed underneath him. He's still naked with only one leg in his jeans. A red welt marks his forehead.

"Oh. My. God," I say. "I'm the worst mother ever."

"Because you had sex with your kid in the house?"

I nod.

"What does that make moms who sex up their husbands? Are they awful, too?"

"No, they're married so they're allowed."

He rolls his eyes and slides his other leg into his pants. "What are you doing later today?" He gives me that sexy boyish grin of his.

This was too close a call. I can't have Tyler walking in on me with a man in my bed. Especially one who isn't going to be around after next week. "We're done. We've maxed out on our one-night stands. You leave at the end of the week so we should just part ways today."

He tugs his T-shirt on. "That's a stupid idea."

"I'm not a pitstop, Dax. I can do one night and walk away. I can't do five or seven or however many nights, start to get attached, and then have you run off to your NFL life. It's not just me—there's Tyler. If you keep coming around and then just disappear, it'll break his heart."

"A pit stop is NASCAR. And technically one night could be considered a pit—"

I grunt in frustration, interrupting him. "Fine. I'm not the halftime entertainment."

He gives me a toothy smile. "You'd be awesome as half-time entertainment. How about a wardrobe malfunction?" He reaches for the belt on my robe and loosens the knot.

I slap at his hand.

"C'mon, babe. Let's spend this week together. Hang out. We don't have to have sex. We can if we want, but it's not mandatory. I'm not going to turn you down. But I'm not gonna stop coming around if you say no sex."

"It's hard to keep things no-strings if we get used to you being around." It's as close to the truth as I can get. I like having him here. I'm mindful that he's gonna ride away in a few days, and that's probably the last time we'll see him. He'll get busy and forget all about us.

He steps out of the closet and sits on the edge of my bed,

then pulls on his socks. "I know this is gonna be hard to believe, but I could use a friend right now."

"And I can be a friend."

"But?" he says, looking up at me.

I sit next to him. "But it's like we've skipped some steps. We're friends who have sex, yet I know nothing about you or your life now. Only what *Bleacher Report* tells me."

He grins. "You looked me up on *Bleacher*?"

I search his face for something, I don't know what. All I know is that when I bring up the future, life after this week, he deflects with jokes. "I only looked you up once, after you left so unexpectedly following that call." Which is not entirely true. I only looked him up once that day. Dax is someone I follow up on periodically.

"Heather, you know how superstitious I am. I don't want to talk about the call until things are solid. If I share too soon, I might jinx it."

Caught off guard by the sudden flash of memory regarding Dax's superstitious nature, I laugh. Of all the things I remembered about Dax, how had I forgotten how superstitious he was? Always tight-lipped until whatever he was sitting on was decided.

No surprise that this was a large part of our breakup. Sure, I understand the need to have all the information before sharing, but I don't understand making big life decisions that affect others without consulting them.

And now I know the call was about work.

I say, "Remember when you learned The Pioneers were hoping to draft you in the first round? You and your dad sat on that info for a few weeks."

He nods. "Because there's no way of knowing what's going to happen. Last minute trades to move up in the draft could have affected where I landed. Unless you're going number one, it's anyone's guess what comes after."

I take his hand. "I get that. But not once during that time did we talk about all the options and where that left us. I find out you're going across the country by watching it on TV like the rest of the football world."

"And you think that'll happen again? Now?"

"It kinda feels like it's already happening. And we aren't even dating. And if we're friends, wouldn't you want to talk it out with me, as your friend? I get a job offer, and my friends are here immediately, helping me figure out the logistics. You're here helping, too. But that flow doesn't seem to be going both ways."

He sighs. "I'm just so used to keeping everything so tight that sharing is hard."

"I get that, But not sharing leaves people guessing. I had no idea what the plan was back then. It left me wondering what you thought of me, of us."

He looks me in the eye. "So you dumped me."

"I got a jump on the inevitable. Your dad was right. You had big plans, and a girlfriend wasn't in them. I was scared, hurt, and angry, and I was determined to dump you before you dumped me."

"My dad told you that? When?"

I look up, trying to recall the timeline. "The day after the draft. I was working at the gym. We hadn't had a chance to talk yet. You were swamped with press things. Your dad came to the gym, and we had a conversation."

"And that night you ended it."

I lean into him and put my head on his shoulder. "Tell me I did the right thing?" Because it felt awful for years after.

Dax kisses my forehead. "We'll never know. What I do

know is that I wasn't planning on ending things. But, yeah, it would have been hard for us to be long-distance. My first year was a ballbuster."

We sit in silence for a beat.

"Having you around has been nice," I say.

"There's that 'nice' word again." He chuckles.

"But where's the meaning of it if we aren't really being friends? If I weren't a single mom and my life looked different, I'd be game for no-strings sex. You've got skill."

His chest puffs out.

"But if you were to leave today, I would question the sincerity of this... whatever we're calling it. Does that make sense? If we left it at the one night, if we really kept it no strings, then the expectations wouldn't be there. But this feels like it's more. You talk about friendship, and that creates a different expectation, at least for me."

"I get it," Dax says. Then, "Last time, a communication problem put us both on unexpected paths."

"Me more than you," I say.

"Funny, though. I look around at what you have and think you got the better end of the deal."

CHAPTER 14

TUESDAY AFTERNOON

"You're a fool," Josie says as she holds the ladder still.

It's after work and we're in my garage, talking about how the morning ended. When Dax left, I had the feeling we wouldn't see him again. We should have left it at the one night. Because watching him ride away made me sad.

I knew if he kept coming around, this feeling would be inevitable. And I try to convince myself that Dax not coming back is for the best.

I stare up at the garage door opener and have no clue how to fix it. I've watched a few YouTube videos, but still I'm clueless. I'm only up here because I need a distraction from my thoughts.

A pang of doubt comes over me. Is Josie right? Am I fool?

I shake my head. Nope. No way. She's crazy.

I tell her as much. "Thing is, yeah, I can be friends with him. But let's define that."

"You never needed our friendship defined."

"I'm not sleeping with you. No chance you can knock me up."

She lets out a string of colorful words. "Just let things happen. Have sex. Don't have sex. Let him share. Don't let him share. Who cares? Unless there's another reason you're fighting this."

Yeah, there's another reason. Not one I want to say out loud anytime soon. Dax is someone I could easily become attached to. Dax not getting attached to me would be devastating. It took years for me to get over him the first time. What if I can't get over him a second time?

I pull a lever on the opener, and nothing happens. The part of me having a pity party would see that as a metaphor for my life.

"I dunno, Jo. My gut says I should tread carefully."

She clears her throat. "The chemistry is still there between you two. We all saw and felt it. And I think you're letting fear dictate everything."

I turn on the ladder, sit on one of the steps, and look down at her. "I think this entire conversation is moot. The way he said goodbye this morning makes me think I won't see him again. And if I'm right, then I did make the right decision. But for giggles, let's play this out. What if he did hang around a lot? And our relationship is classified as 'just friends'. Great. No biggie. But what if it develops into more? I did an internet search on him this morning, and *Bleacher Report* says he's the top candidate to fill the offensive line coach position for the Tampa team. His dad's the head coach there. If that was what the call was about, why wouldn't he just say that? It's not like he could jinx getting hired by his dad."

She shrugs. "Tampa's not a terrible commute. It's not like being across the country."

I shake my head. "Football season is hectic. Even if we

were in the same town, I'd only see him early in the morning or late at night. He'll basically live at the training facility. He'd be gone a lot. I just don't see it working out."

She meets my gaze. "All sound arguments. I can see why you think you've made the right decision where he's concerned. I remember feeling like that after the hurricane destroyed Brinn's flight school and my apartment."

"So, you understand."

She nods. "Which is why I think you're a fool."

I chuckle. "Annnddd we've come full circle."

She grins back. "And the garage door is…"

I jerk my thumb behind to gesture to the garage door opener. "Still broken. And I have no idea how to fix this thing."

"I didn't think you did. But I love you for trying." She smiles.

The rumble of a motorcycle has Josie stepping out of the garage to look down the road.

"Um, how you gonna handle it if he comes back? Because here he comes, and maybe it's the concussions, but he looks ready for round two."

"If he's in a leather jacket, jeans, and biker boots, that's what he always wears when he rides."

"I'm talking about the determined expression on his face."

We watch in silence as Dax cruises into my driveway. I'm not going to lie. Seeing him approach makes my stomach flutter with nervous excitement. My body betrays me every time Dax is around.

He moves slowly as he kicks his long leg over the motor-cycle to stand. I'm not one who generally gets all hot and bothered around bikers, but Dax on a bike in tight jeans works for me. Works for me on all levels. Darn him.

He slides his helmet off and rests it on the seat, then runs a hand through his hair. He smiles at Josie, but his smile falls when he looks at me.

He says, "All right, I've been thinking. I don't want a repeat of what happened in college. I don't want to walk away from here thinking things could be different if we'd communicated better. Also, I came prepared to fix things around here." From his jacket pocket, he pulls out a small pack of light bulbs.

Josie points to it. "Microwave. Nice."

I say, "I don't need you to fix things around my house." I'm holding a screwdriver, and I tap it against my palm.

He points to the garage door opener. "So that works now?"

"Yes," I say.

"No," Josie says. "But darn it if she didn't try."

Because she's still standing slightly below me, I'm able to kick her. Which I do. Right in the shoulder.

"Ow." She looks at me over her shoulder, but she's not scowling. She's smiling. "I should leave so you two can hash this out. I can take Tyler with me to give you plenty of time." She turns to face me and winks. Then mouths "go for it" as she's backing up.

She asks, "Am I taking Tyler?" She gestures to the house.

I shake my head. "Doug wants to take him to a flag football event at the local park. Against my better judgement, I agreed."

She gives me two thumbs-up. As she walks by Dax, she pats his back. I'm sure she says something too, but I can't make it out. Then she gets in her car and drives away.

I climb down the ladder then face him, waiting for him to say whatever it is that made him come back.

He blows out a breath. "That call was from my agent. I have a couple offers on the table, but nothing really appealing. So on Saturday I asked him to put some feelers out. See if maybe there might be another opportunity we didn't consider before."

"Do you really think telling me this might jinx whatever opportunity your agent brought you?"

He gives a boyish shrug. "You can take the boy out of the locker room, but you can't take the locker room superstition out of the boy. I've been this way since Pop Warner football in first grade."

"Fair enough. Then your agent called because...?"

"Because something new popped up, and he wanted me to meet and have a casual conversation with the interested team."

I wag my brows. "Ooohh, so it *was* a team. Ah ha. A clue. You'd better stop there. You're telling me too much."

He gives me a light shove. "Stop making fun of me."

"Dax, the good things that happen to you aren't because you wear the same socks four days in a row, or whatever. It's because you're good at what you do."

"Is this a right step in the direction of friendship?"

I nod. "You have to understand that letting you in is hard for me, too. Letting anyone in is."

He swipes a hand down his face. "Since leaving the NFL, I've floated around, trying to figure out what's next. And for three months now, I haven't come up with one single thing of interest. Until I saw you. I can't stop thinking about you, Heather. When I think of how I want to spend my day, I think of spending it with you."

His declaration warms me to my core. And scares me, too. Being with Dax is easy. It feels natural and right. Which is why I fight him so hard. To lose a connection like this again, I just don't know if I could take it. All these years later, what haunts me the most about our previous time together is the loss of our easy relationship.

I open my mouth to speak, but he puts up a hand to stop me.

He says, "I understand your concern for Tyler. I don't take his part in this lightly. I'm not out to hurt him."

"Promise me you won't just vanish from his life. It *will* hurt him."

"With today's technology, I can't imagine suddenly disappearing. No matter where I am, I can talk with him. Still be his friend. I'm not saying this to be mean, but I'm not like his dad. I value time with him. I value time with you, and with all the people I care about, like my sister and her kids. The people in my life are important to me. I want you both in my life, however that may look. I have no idea what lies ahead for me. I thought I'd still be playing in the NFL. But here I am. And don't take that wrong because I like being here."

Dax approaches and stops right in front of me. He stares at me, searching my face. Then he strokes my cheek. Witless, once again overruled by my body, I go loosey-goosey, barely hanging on to the tool in my hand.

I say, "*Bleacher Report* has you taking a job with your dad's team."

His lips quirk, making his lopsided smile. "Can you imagine being fired by your dad? That would make Christmas awkward. Besides, you know how difficult my dad is. Does that sound like a good career move to you?"

I move to stand by Justin's work table. Not that he ever

used it. And set the screwdriver down. "But you'd be back in the game. You love the game."

He nods. "Yeah, but I love being healthy, too. That's why I quit before I had to. I love not always being stressed out. Working for my dad would be a layer of stress I'm not sure I want."

"Then you aren't going to work for the Tampa team?"

"I wasn't planning on it."

"This is good," I say as I lean against the counter. "A real conversation between friends."

"Who have sex," he adds as he moves closer.

I lean forward enough to lightly punch him in the stomach.

He doubles over in pretend agony. When he looks up at me, his smile big, he says, "Heather, if I had one wish right now, it would be for another day with you."

I want to say yes so desperately I can't think of any more arguments for no.

CHAPTER 15

TUESDAY AFTERNOON

"Okay," I say. "Stay."

He's next to me in a flash and backs me up to the table. "I was gearing up for strong resistance."

"I can give you some if you want." My backside is pressed against the hard wood. "But I wasn't saying okay to hanky-panky."

"But you're not saying no."

Dax lifts me so I'm sitting on the counter. He steps between my legs. I wrap them around him.

"I was hoping for a fight so we could have crazy make-up sex," he says.

He lowers his head to my neck where his lips brush against the sensitive spot below my ear. I run my hands up his chest and circle around his neck, bringing him in closer.

"Wow, that's really presumptive. Assuming I'll jump in bed with you anywhere, anytime," I tease.

He pushes away and steps back. "You're right. You're right." He rubs a hand down his face. "And with Tyler in the house, too."

I hold up my hands in surprise. "I was kidding."

He shakes his head. "Nope, you're right." He watches me closely as he leans forward then slowly slides the screwdriver off the counter. A smile twitches on his lips.

He says, "I'll just fix this up, and then we can go inside and figure out something to do. Or just hang out."

He moves to the ladder and, in a flash, is three rungs up and has the cover of the door opener removed. He messes with a few cables and lines, or whatever they're called, then gives me his attention. "You got the remote on you?"

I nod and take it from where I clipped it on the side of my jeans.

"Give it a press," he says.

I click the button, and the garage door closes. Thankfully, the high row of twelve by twelve widows on my east-facing wall lets in copious amounts of light so we're not left in the dark.

I squeal in delight. "That's awesome. Don't tell me how easy it was, please. I'm just gonna sit here and enjoy the fact that it works."

He hops off the ladder and strolls over to me with a cowboy's swagger. He flips the screwdriver once in the air, catches it, then slides it in his front pocket like a gun going into a holster.

"Fixing that dohickey there was complicated man's work, little lady," he says with a drawl.

I laugh. "How ever will I repay you?" I use my best southern accent and pretend to fan myself.

"Well, ma'am. I could never take any of your money...." He tips his pretend cowboy hat.

Our goofy exchange makes me hot. Maybe it's because he's so willing to be silly. Or the fact that he just made coming home safer for me and Tyler since we'll now be able to park in our garage.

I go right for what I want. No more playing this game or any other. "How about a quickie in the garage?" I propose. I strip off my T-shirt.

His eyes go wide. He whips the screwdriver from his pants and drops it on the ground. "Yes, please," he says and rushes me.

He draws me in close, sliding his hands under my butt. I'm pressed against him, and everything feels like it should.

He blazes a path of kisses down my neck and up again before he stops to nuzzle my collarbone, his lips spread wide in what I know is a smile. "Everything about you feels right."

I was thinking the same thing. I kiss him under his chin, knowing this spot is his favorite.

He groans. "What about Tyler?"

And I love that he thinks about my kid.

"He's deep into Ninja Turtles." I glance at my watch. "We have about fifteen minutes before they end and he comes looking for more food."

"Fifteen, got it."

Dax's hands go to the waist of my jean shorts. He pauses. "Is this okay? Out here?"

My answer is to undo his jeans and lower the zipper.

"We need a blanket," he says.

To the side is a shelf where I store a picnic blanket. I point to it, and Dax grabs it and with my help, lays it out on the workbench surface. He lifts me and sets me on the blanket.

We're fast and to the point, though some might not find it romantic that his pants are down to his knees and mine are on the floor. But his touch is gentle and caring, his kisses are warm and lingering. And when I roll on the condom, we stare into each other's eyes breathing fast and heavy because one second feels like an eternity and we need be connected now. I feel like the center of the universe as he loves me right over the edge into a blissful release, and I hold on to him with all I have. Never wanting to let go.

CHAPTER 16
TUESDAY EVENING

Tyler is over the moon that Dax is hanging out at our house. And that the microwave has a working light so he can now watch the popcorn bag get bigger and bigger as it pops.

Kids and their simple pleasures.

I'm over the moon that after our tryst in the garage, Dax cleaned out my gutter. No more water pooling. I thought I had a roof leak, but it turned out to be something simpler and easier to fix.

And I don't overthink the fact that a pro football dude stands in my kitchen making all of us grilled cheese sandwiches for dinner while cracking fart jokes with Tyler. Because to me, it's just Dax. We've slipped right back into how we used to be together. Only this time, it's better.

"We should go to the beach," Dax says and flips the sandwich by tossing it in the air and catching it in the pan.

Tyler's in awe. "Can't," he says, staring at Dax like he's a magician. "Uncle Doug is taking me to a flag football game down at the park. It's for kids my age, and Mom says I can play."

Dax nods and smiles. "That's right. Your mom said something about that. Then dude, we should totally *not* go to the beach. Football is way more important."

Tyler nods in agreement. I snort to show I disagree.

Dax asks me, "Are you going, too?"

I shake my head. "I think I might kill the fun vibe if I was there."

Dax slides a sandwich onto Tyler's plate.

Tyler says, "She worries a lot."

"Yes, she does," Dax agrees.

I put chips on Tyler's plate. "I worry because I love you."

But Ty's forgotten about me. He's cramming the sandwich in his mouth like a man with his last meal.

I put a hand on his shoulder. "Slow down. You have time."

Dax tosses a second sandwich in the air and says to me, "What are you going to do with the boys gone?"

"You're going?" I kinda figured he'd stay with me and we'd play NFL player and naughty cheerleader. I'd even let him be the NFL player if he wanted.

"If Tyler will let me."

"Yeah!" Food particles fly out of Tyler's mouth in his haste to assure Dax that he's welcome.

"Maybe after football, we can all go get ice cream?" Dax says. He meets my gaze over Tyler's head and raises a brow asking if his offer is okay. But too late now.

Tyler gives Dax two thumbs-up. "Can we go to that place where you put the ice cream in a cup and add your own toppings? We only do that on special occasions."

Dax ruffles Tyler's hair. "That's what this is. A special occasion. You're getting to play football today."

Tyler pumps his fist and then looks at me with uncertainty. "It's still okay, right?"

I nod and smile. Even though I want to say no. I'd rather he build Legos or do his homework. Something safer. "We won't be able to stay out too late. It's a school night."

He rushes to hug me, and I fold him into my arms and hold tight.

"What are you going to do while the men are out playing sports?" Dax asks as he sits at the table, all the sandwiches done.

I release Tyler and move to put chips on our plates. "I heard back from my college advisor. To switch my degree to be a child life specialist, I need only two more classes, so I want to register for those. I need to get ready for finals in May."

Tyler makes a face. "School at night. No way."

I chuckle. "I kinda like it. And I can get it done today without any interruptions," I tease and poke him in the belly.

We talk about Tyler's dream of making a grand play, and Dax shares how he thought he was going to make one in a big game and tripped over his own feet. His message to Tyler being that there's always another day to do something grand.

To which Tyler replies, "I might only have today." And punctuates it with a sad look filled with dreams unachieved.

"I make no promises, but if today goes well," I say, "then we can talk about next week, too."

Tyler and Dax pound fists and Tyler runs off to get his football stuff together. 'Stuff' being a flag football belt he wore when he and my brother played in the back yard.

"You're a good mom," Dax says between shoving chips in his face.

"Maybe. Maybe being overprotective will have negative consequences I can't foresee."

"Maybe. But doubtful. Doug and I'll will make sure he's okay."

"I know," I say. Trouble is, I'm just the right amount of a control freak that I believe only I can make sure Tyler's okay to the degree I need him to be.

Doug arrives thirty minutes later. He's only mildly surprised to see Dax. Probably because my mom already filled him in on Dax showing up the other day.

My brother and I didn't go to the same college, so Doug only knew Dax from brief exchanges when he would come down to my university to watch games.

"Where's your van?" he asks me as he's shaking Dax's hand.

"In the garage."

"Dax fixed the opener," Tyler says.

Doug says to Dax, "I didn't even know it wasn't working."

As if it should matter that Doug needed to explain to Dax why he hadn't fixed everything in my house.

I roll my eyes.

"I wouldn't have known it wasn't working either if her friends hadn't mentioned it." Dax places a hand on my shoulder. The gesture makes a statement, whether it be that our relationship is familiar or he's being possessive. Unnecessary, yet neither feels wrong. "It's not like she *asks* for help."

Doug nods. "She gets her stubborn streak from our dad."

Our dad is not the most warm and loving father. He works from the premise that if he rules like an authoritarian, then we'll be good little subjects and do everything by the book. Guess I proved him wrong on that.

Tyler tugs at Doug's hand. "Is it time to go?"

"In five minutes, Bubba. We need to get some water for you and sunscreen and—"

I hand him a backpack tha was leaning against the wall. "It's all in here. Even his doctor's emergency numbers. If something—"

Doug puts a hand up to stop me. "I know. We've been through this one thousand times. I'm prepared. I know the drill. I'll take really good care of him."

And he will. Because my brother has been wanting his own child for several years and keeps meeting a brick wall. He loves Tyler and would never be careless or neglectful.

"I trust you," I say. "One day you'll be a great dad because you're an amazing uncle."

Doug smiles. "I'm not supposed to say anything. Kenley wants to tell you and the girls, but there's a young woman, seventeen, who is having a baby and wants to do an open adoption. She liked our bios and has selected us. This is the one time having an interracial marriage has worked to our benefit."

Tears of joy spring to my eyes. "Doug, that's fantastic!" I fan my face to keep the tears from falling. "I'm so happy for you two."

He points to my face. "Make sure you have that reaction when she tells you."

I wrap him in a hug. "I love you, and I can't wait to give you a hard time about all those sleepless nights coming. It'll be awesome."

Doug groans and pushes me away, moisture in his eyes. "C'mon Tyler. Let's go play some football."

Tyler gives me a quick hug and is out the door, followed by Doug with the backpack.

Dax pauses before exiting. "Enjoy your quiet. We got this." He winks and steps out.

It takes a good thirty minutes before I can focus on my To Do list. I register for the classes, organize my class notes, and make a few flashcards, which I use to help me study, so I can be ready for finals.

An hour later, I'm painting my toenails when my cell rings. Doug's name shows up on the screen.

My first words are, "So, how was it? Everything he expected and more? Though I'll admit I hope he kinda hated it."

"Heather," Doug says in a tone that makes me sit up straight.

"Oh my god, what's happened?"

"There's nothing to freak out about. Everyone's okay. We're at Halifax Medical Center in the emergency room—"

Simultaneously, I disconnect and spring up. There's no point in hearing whatever it is Doug has to say. Because I'll only be able to deal with it once I see it for myself.

Sliding my feet in flip-flops and not caring about the wet polish, I grab my purse and dash outside. Only my van's in the garage and the remote is inside. I cuss Dax and his handyman skills and, with fumbling hands, get the front door unlocked. I dash through the kitchen and out the door to the garage, slamming my palm against the wall-mounted clicker that opens the door.

My breathing is shallow. My heart is racing. I glance at my watch and tap the screen, wondering why it didn't give me an alert. Tyler's seizures can be ugly. And they ravage him. Afterward, he'll sometimes throw up or collapse from exhaustion. All of which is manageable. But to have to go to the emergency room tells me this is big. Too big. And no alert on my watch means it might not be a seizure. My mind races with all the awful possibilities.

I speed down the street, not even sure I closed the garage. My knees shake as I make the ten-mile drive from the beachside of Daytona to the mainland toward the hospital.

"Please let him be okay," is all I can say.

CHAPTER 17

TUESDAY NIGHT

ADHERING TO THE MUNDANE BUT NECESSARY LAWS OF operating a vehicle and using the roadways -- stopping at red lights, not tailgating, and parking in a legal spot -- is a certain form of torture.

My kid is in the emergency room, and having to be law-abiding is asking too much from me. I speed as I cross over from the peninsula to the mainland. And in my haste in taking a corner, I cut it sharply and jump a curb.

Finally, I arrive. I park in the first spot I find then sprint to the emergency department. I pause just inside the sliding doors and scan the room. I spot Dax leaning against the counter of the nurse's station, chatting with a guy in a long white lab coat and a stethoscope around his neck, and two nurses in teal scrubs. They're laughing at whatever he's telling them.

My blood pressure shoots through the roof, and I see red. Literally. A red overlay of color, brought on by my fury, tints the world in front of me. All I can hear is the sound of my breathing combined with my rapidly thumping heartbeat.

I stomp toward Dax. When he sees me,] he smiles and waves.

"Where is he?" My voice quivers from pent up anger and fear. My volume louder than normal.

"He's with Doug." Dax looks confused.

The nurses' station separates us. I slap my hand on the laminate surface. "You said you'd take care of him. You said he'd be okay. Someone take me to my child," I fairly scream.

From behind me, Tyler says, "I'm right here, Mom."

I turn, bracing myself, because I have no idea what I'll see.

My son is riding my brother's shoulders. He's holding a balloon that says *Get well soon*. He looks fine. He looks healthy. There's a streak of dirt on his cheek, but nothing else amiss.

I sag with relief. "What happened?"

Doug lifts Tyler off his shoulders and sets him on the ground. "If you hadn't hung up on me, I would've told you."

Tyler skirts around me and runs to Dax. "This is for you." He hands him the balloon.

I'm confused. I try to put the pieces of this puzzle together, only it seems I've grabbed the wrong ones. Dax hops from around the counter to get closer to Tyler.

"I love balloons," Dax says.

On his right lower leg is a brace acting as a temporary cast that goes from his ankle to slightly above his knee. The brace's slight bend at the knee keeps Dax's foot from touching the ground.

I gasp. "You? You're the one that's hurt? Not Tyler?" My question is rhetorical, yet affirmation would go a long way. Even though I can see Tyler is fine, my brain hasn't made the switch to accepting it yet.

"Yeah, ding-dong," Doug says. "Dax has a tibial fracture."

I gasp again and cover my mouth. Between my fingers, I say, "Didn't you break your tibia junior year of college?" We hadn't been dating, but I remember the story and how he'd rehabbed for so long, afraid an injury would keep him from the draft.

"Yep, this one's not in the same spot, though. This fracture is on the tibial shaft." He nods to the doctor. "This guy called it a toddler fracture. That makes me feel big and strong."

He takes the balloon from Tyler. "Thanks, buddy, you were such a good friend when I stepped in that hole. Means a lot to me that you were with me the whole time." He wraps Tyler in a hug.

I face Doug and give him a look that tells him to fill me in.

Doug shrugs. "Tyler got the ball and was running it in. First touchdown of the game and for Tyler. Dax was running down the field on the sidelines with him, cheering him along."

Dax laughs. "Yeah, only I was running backward and not watching where I was going."

Doug says, "Stepped right into a hole and fell back."

"Snap," Tyler says. "We all heard it."

Dax adds, "I think it's the beginning of a sinkhole. Sucked me right in and wouldn't let go."

I clasp my hands to my cheeks. "I'm sorry I accused you. I—"

Dax holds up his hand as he straightens. "I get it. Let's get out of here. The pain meds are kicking in and making me tired."

The doctor reminds Dax of his weight-bearing restrictions and his follow-up orthopedic appointment. He thanks Dax for his autograph. An orderly comes out from a room marked Storage holding crutches.

"Finally found some big enough," he says and hands them to Dax. "But you still have to ride the wheelchair out of here."

"Let me go pull up the van," I say. "Come on, Tyler."

"I'll wait with Dax," he says, and takes Dax's hand.

I nod, cast Dax an uncertain look, feeling as if my apology wasn't enough, and wanting to say more, but after a moment's hesitation, I head outside to bring the van around.

We get Dax tucked into the minivan and Doug says to Tyler, "I'll send your mom the video of your touchdown. Well done, kiddo." They tap fists. Tyler beams.

Dax says, "I can't wait to see the part where I go down."

"It's priceless, dude." Doug gives Dax a slap on the shoulder, then walks away.

I pause, with my hand on the gear shifter, "Where are you staying?"

"Hotel on the beach." Dax reclines his seat and closes his eyes.

"Where do you live right now?" I can't believe I don't know the answer.

"I was staying at my parents'. I haven't looked into real estate since I wasn't sure where I would land." His voice is quiet as if he's about to drift off.

"You can't stay in a hotel by yourself." I'm thinking through the options.

"Please don't make my mommy come and get me," Dax says with a laugh.

"You can stay with us." Taking care of him would assuage me of my guilt to a degree.

"That would be awesome," Tyler says.

Dax puts his thumbs up.

"Let's go by your hotel and get your stuff," I suggest.

Dax cracks an eye open. "I don't have the energy to get out of this car but one time."

"Is it a lot of stuff? I can go grab everything really quick. Unless you'd rather I didn't."

Still with one eye open Dax says, "You mean check out and stay with you?"

I nod and resist rolling my eyes. "Yeah, that's what 'stay with us' means. Somehow I don't think you'll magically heal by tomorrow and be able to get on your bike and go about your business."

Tyler adds, "In our house when you're sick, Mom gives you the ironing board."

Both of Dax's eyes are open now and he looks over his shoulder at Tyler, wincing slightly from the move. "That sounds awful. Maybe you *should* call my mom."

Tyler laughs. "No, it means you can be on the couch with the ironing board next to you. It's loaded with all your favorite foods, and you get all the TV you can watch."

Dax smiles at me. "Sounds like heaven. Sign me up." He falls back against the seat, then digs in his front pocket. The right leg of his jeans has been cut off at the knee and he looks like a hot mess. His elbow is scraped, there's a tear in the right shoulder of his shirt, and dirt on that side.

From his pocket, he pulls out his hotel key and hands it to me. I stick it in the cup holder and head back across the bridge to the beachside.

An hour later, we're back at my house with Dax tucked in on the couch. I had to cut his jeans off him entirely. He's now wearing baggy athletic shorts and a clean T-shirt, and snoring softly.

After a shower, I get Tyler to bed. It not until he's breathing evenly in a sound sleep that I take a deep, freeing breath. He's okay. Dax is okay. Everyone is okay. My nerves are shot.

For what's likely the tenth time, I watch the video Doug sent me of Tyler running to make a touchdown and Dax running backwards down the field cheering him on. My heart swells. His affection for Tyler is clear. I'm relieved because my attachment to Dax grows by the minute. And that comes with a fresh fear I'm not sure I know how to manage.

CHAPTER 18

LATE TUESDAY NIGHT

"Why are you standing there looking scared and worrying your hands?" Dax stretches on the couch while watching me.

I went into the living room to check on him and take an extra blanket, only to find him awake. Midnight is fast approaching.

All evening, I've felt like a horse's ass for my behavior at the hospital. Besides owing Dax an apology, I want to make sure he understands my reaction. He seems chilled, but he's also medicated.

I stand at the end of the couch near his feet, still dressed in my cutoff shorts and T-shirt. My toenail polish from this afternoon looks like a hack job, smeared and chipped. "I was awful to you. I rushed in and jumped your case. I made a bad assumption."

He nods. "You were awful."

I clasp my hands to my face in horror. "Was I really?"

"You just said you were."

"But I thought you'd disagree with me."

"Would you believe me if I did?"

I shake my head.

He does a one shoulder shrug. "There you go. So let's just move on from it because nothing I say will make you think otherwise. I'd rather talk about how you can make it up to me."

I take in a deep breath. Humiliation from my earlier behavior spreads across my chest like a light sunburn, leaving my chest feeling warm, the red blotches blossoming. "You mean, more than letting you stay here and catering to you?"

Dax's narrowed eyes and pressed lips tell me he's considering my response. Then he says, "Yeah, other than that. Tell me. Were you scared when you saw I was injured?"

I move to sit on the arm of the couch, my feet on the cushion. "No. I was relieved it wasn't Tyler."

Dax frowns. "That doesn't make me feel good. Lie and tell me it terrified you."

I laugh. "When I came in, you were joking with the doctor and nurses. I knew you were okay."

"Fair point."

I confess something I'd been holding back from him. "But that away game last year, when you played the Chargers and you took that hit from their safety, I was scared then. You went down like a sack of rocks and didn't move. Those were the longest minutes of any game I've ever watched."

He looks pleased. "Did you watch all my games?"

I shrug as if it's neither here nor there. "I watch a lot of football. Sometimes it was a game you were in, and sometimes it wasn't." No lie there. Only I omitted that I watched as many of his games as I could.

He seems only slightly satisfied. "I would've been scared,

too, in that game, if I'd been conscious. When I came to, I was confused. I knew something was wrong."

"I really wanted you to let them cart you off."

He tucks his hands behind his head. "I had the wherewithal to know if I did that, I was definitely sitting out for several games."

"Which wouldn't have been a bad thing," I point out.

"In hindsight," he says with a smile. Because seven games later he sustained another concussion.

"Was it that last one that clinched the deal, made you get out?" I tuck the tips of my toes between the cushions.

He rubs a hand over his face then puts it behind his head. "It was a couple of things. The first was, I struggled to remember the playbook. The second, my parents happened to be in town for that game where I got my last concussion. My mom brought pictures of my sister's kids, and I couldn't remember their names." He makes a point of making eye contact. "They're seven and four. I've had plenty of time to remember their names."

The balloon Tyler gave him is weighed down by a heavy plastic heart tied to the string. It floats by the couch and I play with the string, making it bounce up and down. "And anything else? Not that losing your memory wasn't enough." But I knew Dax. I knew something else had scared him.

"I was at practice, and we were going through a play. One we'd done several times. One of the guys was having a hard time, or maybe it was me. I don't know. But I lost my cool. Said some ugly things and ended up in a slugfest with him." He shakes his head with regret. "Thing is, I liked this guy. Never had a problem with him before. Afterward, he said something off-hand about not being myself. I went to the doctor, and he said I was staring down a barrel at long-term brain issues if I got any more serious head injuries."

"I never heard about a fight between you and a teammate." The team had done a good job keeping it out of the press.

He wags his brows "Following me, were you?"

I roll my eyes. "Okay, one wish."

He glances over the back of the couch at where the bedrooms are. Then looks back at me. "For you to get naked."

Tyler's out like a light. He had a full day, too. He fell asleep seconds after his head hit the pillow, and I closed his door to keep from waking him. Question is, will I be comfortable having sexy time in the living room where, if Tyler suddenly woke and came out, we'd get busted?

No, I might not be fully comfortable, but I'm willing to give it a go. I need to be close to Dax, to hold him and show him I'm thankful he's okay. That today's emergency was manageable.

And, weirdly, the relief that followed the fear that my child had been hurt makes me want to experience life on a more thrilling level. Maybe to prove life isn't so precarious after all.

I tug the balloon down and twist off the plastic stop that keeps the helium in. I put the balloon end to my mouth and suck in.

In a Minnie Mouse voice, I say, "What would you like me to take off first?" I stand, one hand thrust out to the side and gesture up and down my body. It takes everything I have not to laugh.

But Dax does. He sits up quickly, winces, but gestures for me to hand him the balloon. I do.

He sucks in some helium. "Girl, I don't care. Just take it all off because I love looking at every part of you." His words are sweet, but the altered voice makes them silly, and I laugh.

I take back the balloon, pinching the tip between my fingers. I unfasten the button on my jean shorts and shrug them to where they're riding low on my hips. Then I take in a hit of helium.

"You just lay there and enjoy the ride, mister," I say. "Because this is what I have planned." I have to take a second hit of helium to go into the details. There's absolutely nothing sexy about the high, squeaky pitch of my voice. But there is something tantalizing about telling each other what we want and what we plan to do. Who cares how it sounds?

He gestures for his turn. Before he takes in any helium. , he says, "I'm hard as a rock. Should I worry that even with a squeaky Minnie Mouse voice, I find you so goddamn sexy?"

I let my shorts fall to the floor and then climb on top of him, mindful of his brace. I straddle him.

He takes in helium. In a squeaky voice, he says, "Take your shirt off, please. Pretty please."

We laugh. The balloon is empty. He tosses it aside. Going slow, I pull my shirt over my head. He removes my bra.

"I'll happily break both legs if I can get this again."

"We haven't done anything yet," I say.

"No, but I already know it's going to be amazing. I sure wish you'd been there when I came to after those concussions."

His hands are on my boobs and mine are on the elastic of his shorts.

He suddenly grabs my hands and goes still. "Wait, Tyler? Are you sure he's asleep?"

When he considers my child, my feelings for him grow even stronger.

"He's asleep, and he's generally a sound sleeper. If he has a seizure, we'll hear an alarm." I tap my watch. "And this will warn us."

He nods slightly as if considering what we're about to do. "Okay, but let's make it quick."

I laugh and get back to undressing him.

There's nothing quick about our lovemaking. With me on top, I have full control. I tease as I caress my body against his. And without words, using our hands and bodies to express our needs and feelings, I take him in slowly and fully.

He groans.

I gently ride him, keeping my strokes rhythmical, each one bringing us closer to the precipice of pleasure.

As we reach our climax together he sits up, pushing deeper inside me, wraps his arms around me, and holds tight.

CHAPTER 19

WEDNESDAY: ONE WEEK LATER

EVERY DAY FOR THE LAST SEVEN DAYS, I REMINDED MYSELF NOT to get used to Dax being around. Even balanced on one crutch, he's helped around the house, and just that little extra opens up enough breathing room for me to get my schoolwork done.

My mom didn't hesitate to turn over after-school care to Dax either. Doug thinks she is testing Dax for staying power. I made sure to tell her he wasn't staying. Last thing I need is Mom dropping off wedding magazines or something equally embarrassing.

I tell her what I know. Dax is here for a few weeks. Truth is, we never talked about why he doesn't have someone come get him and take him to his mom and dad's. Only that he says being at his parents' house is wonderful and hellish at the same time.

The media found out about his accident, and his cell phone has been chiming with emails and ringing off the hook. A few articles question what he was doing at a kid's flag football game, but an unverified source says he was there watching his nephew.

Dax says his agent spread that rumor. I appreciate the anonymity.

Last thing we need or want is media outside my house.

I drive home from work with the universal question on my mind. What am I going to make for dinner?

The downside to Dax staying with us is his appetite is too big for my small budget. Pasta was always an easy way to stretch dollars, but we've had it twice already this week.

When I pull up, Dax is coming from around the house.

I park in the garage, such a wonderful gift, and get out to meet him. He's resting on his crutches behind my van.

I sniff. "Are you grilling?"

"Steaks and shrimp. I had groceries delivered. Sorry, it took me a few days to realize I was eating everything you had."

I wave a hand dismissively like it isn't a big deal, but inside I'm relieved. And embarrassed. Payday is today, so I couldn't shop any earlier.

"It smells so good."

He smiles. "You up for making a salad?"

I toss my purse over my shoulder. "I'd love to." I turn to go, but he grabs me by my elbow.

"Real quick. I want to tell you something out here. I don't want Tyler to hear."

My heart plummets. No matter how hard I try to be realistic, that this week of playing house can't go on forever. Sometimes I've let myself indulge in the fantasy of it.

"This sounds bad," I say, hoping he'll reassure me.

"You tell me. I have an opinion, but I don't want to make snap judgements."

Now I'm concerned. I lean against the workbench and try not to think of us getting hot and bothered all over it. I cross my arms preparing for blows. "Hit me with it."

"Your ex came by today."

Cocking my head, I say, "Justin?"

Dax's lips quirk. "Do you have another?"

"Lord, no. What did he want?"

"To bring you a check." He reaches into his back pocket, then pulls out a folded square of paper and holds it out to me.

I take it and open it. Sure enough, it's a child support check.

Dax says, "Lemme guess. It's not close to what he owes you?"

"Nope, this is one-third of what he owes me for one month, and he's three months behind."

"You need to get your lawyer after him."

I fold the check and leave it on the workbench counter. "In the three years we've been divorced, I've had to do that four times." I hold up four fingers. "You know how much it cost me to have my lawyer make him pay?"

Dax shakes his head.

"Almost a grand. Each time. It's like he does it on purpose just to be a butthead to me."

Dax shifts his weight and rests against my minivan, kicking his broken leg out in front. "Humor me for a minute. What if he is doing it on purpose?"

I laugh because the idea is absurd. Justin couldn't care less about us. "Why? He barely noticed us when we were married. What's his motivation?"

Dax shrugs. "That I don't know, but listen. I'm on the couch watching *Ridiculousness* and telling myself not to take a pain pill even though I want to. Whenever I do, I consume an entire bag of chips and we're out of chips and I don't have training camp coming up so I don't want to put on weight."

I wave my hand to show he needs to speed this up. Though it's cute that he's thinking about his weight.

"Anyway, I hear a noise in the garage, so I put the TV on mute. Then I hear that door open." He points to the interior garage door that leads to my kitchen.

"How is that possible? I lock the exterior door, and the garage door is fixed."

"He had a key. I saw him pocket it when he came in. He hadn't noticed me yet."

I feel sweaty and slightly sick to my stomach. Why would Justin have a key to the house and come in when he knows good and well we aren't home? "What did he do then?"

"Went through your mail. Broke the light to the microwave."

"How'd he do that?"

Dax's lips are pressed thin. He's furious.

In hopes of lightening the mood, I say, "Is he still alive?"

"He's lucky he is," he says. Effort thwarted. "He took the bulb out and shook it until he broke the filament. I just sat there and watched him. I wanted to see what else he was up to."

"And?"

"That's when he came into the living room and saw me. He was holding your laptop. Tried to tell me he comes by to check on things for you every month. Wants to make sure you're all safe."

"But he just broke—" I gesture toward the house.

"Yep, and he knew I knew he'd done it, too. That's when he whipped out his checkbook and said he was also leaving a check. Wanted me to tell you he's sorry it's late, but the first chance he gets, he'll make good."

"Bullshit," I say.

"Here's the thing. When I cleaned out your gutters the other day, the clogs didn't look normal. They looked like someone had packed leaves and rocks and bark in there."

"Rocks?"

"Yeah. To cause the water to pool in that one corner of the house where, with enough exposure, you'll have a leak and bigger issues."

I'm stunned. "None of this makes sense. Why would he do this?"

"I don't know. But I called Doug to ask about the things he's fixed over the years. Justin could be the reason for at least half of those issues."

I shake my head, unable to take in the enormity of what he's suggesting.

Dax gestures for me to follow him. "I have to check on the steaks. But here's another thing. He wasn't happy to see me. Not because I busted him, but I don't think he wants to see you with any man, especially me. He brought up college. Talked about how I let you go, and he won, and that I needed to know when it came time for you to choose, you picked him."

We make our way to the backyard. The hickory smell of the grill is stronger, but even though I was hungry when I arrived, I'm now sick to my stomach. "That doesn't even make sense. I didn't even know him until after we broke up. You were long gone to California when I met Justin."

"I don't think we've seen the last of him." Dax lifts foil off a tray sitting on my outdoor table and puts shrimp on the grill.

My mind races. "I need to have the locks changed. All of them."

"Done," he says. "New keys are on the kitchen table. I also ordered you a camera system, one that will ping your phone." He closes the lid and wraps an arm around me. "But you have me. I'm the best security system there is." He holds out an arm in front of me and flexes, making his bicep jump.

I laugh and swat him away. I don't say that one day Dax might not be here. "I'm going in to make the salad." I need to process all this.

He swats me on the butt when I pass. "Tell Tyler to come out here. I'll teach him how to play with fire safely."

Horrified, I stare at Dax. "I will not!"

He bursts out laughing. "I knew you'd say that."

CHAPTER 20

MONDAY

On Monday, Justin delivers his bomb. I'll give him credit; at least we were able to enjoy the weekend before he made his return visit.

Thankfully, Doug took Tyler back to the park for another flag football game. Dax was trying to convince me to recreate the late-night lovemaking couch scene from last week, only this time in the bedroom. I was half convinced when the doorbell rang.

"Man!" Dax says and hops to the couch. He'll get a boot in two weeks, and he's chomping at the bit for that.

As I open the door I'm chuckling, but my laughter falls flat. Justin stands there looking angry. He's slapping a packet of paper against his palm.

"Took you long enough." He pushes past me into the house, walking straight into the living room.

"Excuse me," I say. "You don't live here anymore. You can't just barge in."

Justin gestures to the space. "I paid for this."

"And you gave it to me in the divorce. Now I pay for it." I gesture to the door.

"I have something to say." He scowls at Dax.

The thing I've learned about Justin is that he's a lot of bluster. He puffs up as a smokescreen, a distraction. Many times, after getting home late, I asked him where he'd been and got the defensive act followed by how-dare-I accuse-him-when-he-supports-me-with-staying-at-home song and dance. I'd long become accustomed to this and could see through it.

"Then say it." I glance at Dax; his lips are pressed into a thin line. He's holding a crutch in one hand as if preparing to use it in a fight.

I also notice Justin has a new hairstyle. His blond hair has been cut to allow for side-swept bangs, making him look younger and like a surfer. A trendier look for a guy who tended to be slightly boring in appearance. Even his dark-washed jeans and T-shirt are more in style.

Justin holds out the packet to me. "This is a court order to have a paternity test done on Tyler. I don't think he's mine, and this will prove it."

Fury makes me snatch the papers from him instead of snatching all the hair off his stupid head. "Whose kid would he be, Justin? Never mind how much he looks like you."

Justin points a long finger at Dax. "His kid, and he can start paying for him. And don't say he looks like me, he looks like you. When it comes back that Tyler isn't mine, I expect full restitution for all the child support money I've given you over the last three years." He crosses his arms and lifts his chin.

"I'm surprised you don't want restitution from the day he was born."

Justin blinks a long one, then says, "My lawyer says I can't get it]."

I lunge at him, but Dax leaps from the couch and catches me before I can get my hands around Justin's throat or any other part of his body.

Dax stands behind me, his arms holding me back.

I say, "I really hope Tyler isn't your kid. By some miracle of conception, I'll take Mickey Mouse for his father over you any day."

"I'll be happy for the truth to come out," Justin says, as if he's taking the high road. "For Tyler's sake."

"Why are you doing this? What happens when the DNA proves you are his father? You gonna start paying what you owe on time then? You know I don't have the money to fight you in court anymore." Though I've stopped trying to get to Justin to kill him, I'm by no means relaxed.

"I'm not worried about that because I'm confident I'm not the father." He points a finger to Dax. "Besides, you got yourself a cash cow there. I gave you everything, and it was never enough because you never got over him. He was always the elephant in the room. Now he's not."

Confused, I say, "I never once compared you to Dax. You're talking like a crazy person."

Justin puffs out his chest as if trying to seem larger than he is. "Maybe you didn't say anything, but I could see your face when we'd watch his games. You'd twirl your hair and smile, and I knew you were thinking of him." He jabs his finger at us again.

Because I'm only human and coming from a place of anger not common sense, I say, "Yeah, I probably was thinking about him. He's so much better than you in bed." On one hand, I hold up my pinky and pretend to measure it with the thumb and index finger of my other hand. Then I pointedly look at Justin's crotch. The message is clear.

Justin's face goes red. "You have forty-eight hours to submit the sample." He storms out.

I break free from Dax and follow him. Outside, I notice he's driving a new car. A BMW XX series.

"This is nice," I say as I skirt past him and run my hand along the shiny black hood, leaving an obvious smudge. In the back seat is not a car seat for his child but a golf bag loaded with clubs.

"Having regrets for quitting me?" Justin smirks.

As if. "Is this why you can't pay child support? Having an ex-wife and a kid to support cramping your style?"

He pushes me away from the car, and I stumble backward.

"Hey, hands off her," Dax yells and makes it across the yard in record time, especially for a man using crutches. He's got Justin backed up against the car and is towering over him. "You can come here and make your request. But you can't come here and put your hands on her or Tyler. Do I make myself clear? I know you've been letting yourself in and breaking things. I don't know why. Maybe you thought she'd call you for help, or maybe you're just an asshole. Either way, it all stops now."

Justin's Adam's apple bobs as he swallows convulsively. "I'll happily let you take them off my hands."

Dax's shoulders broaden. "I'd happily take them."

It's a stare down, and I break the silence.

"Leave, Justin."

He has to slide away from Dax and can only open his door a fraction.

"Here," he says and reaches into the car. He pulls out a

small white box and tosses it to me. I catch it with one hand. The label on the top reads DNA Kit.

"When the label gets scanned at the post office, I'll get confirmation it was submitted. Forty-eight hours." His remarks are directed at me.

"What? You don't want to make sure I don't fudge it somehow. Maybe I have some of your DNA lying around. I could use that." I know I can't and I won't, but this isn't my finest moment. How did I ever marry this man?

"Duh," Justin says. "I already asked that question, too. That would show up as a direct match to me." He gets in his car and slams the door. The locks engaging makes me laugh.

Dax looks over his shoulder at me and rolls his eyes.

Justin pulls away at a quick clip, and I'm happy to see him gone.

I say, "He should be ashamed of himself."

Dax turns and gestures for us to go inside. "Is it even a possibility? Could Tyler be mine?"

We go inside and I close the door, then follow him to the couch. "The last time we slept together was the night before the draft. That was the last week in April."

Dax smiles, pleased I remember. Men!

"I met Justin in July at a party. I'm ashamed to say I slept with him the first night."

One of Dax's brows raises slightly.

"Don't judge me. I was trying to get over you. I never claimed having sex with Justin to be my finest moment. Though I did get Tyler."

Dax sits up and slaps his hand on his knee. "Wait. Back up. You were getting over me? You broke up with me!"

"We've had this conversation. I broke up with you because you were going to break up with me."

"Based on what my dad said. Which was what exactly?" His face is dark with frustration.

I give a half shrug. "He said you had no plans for a long-distance relationship and it would be really hard on you at training camp. You couldn't be distracted."

Dax slaps his hand on his forehead. "And you never thought to ask me about any of that?"

"Was he wrong?" I toss the DNA kit on the coffee table then cross my arms. I'm ready to rumble, having not gotten all my frustration out on Justin. "You said the other morning that training camp was a ball buster."

Dax grimaces. "Not entirely. Yeah, it would've been hard. But I didn't want to break up. I thought maybe we'd just see how it played out. Then you ended it. Out of the blue. I felt blindsided."

Like a balloon that's lost all its air, my anger deflates. "Yeah, that might have been better than my knee-jerk reaction." My snap decision, made without all the facts, sent me down a path I never imagined. The one good outcome? Tyler. I could never have regrets about him. I say, "But you know what would have been the best solution? Talking it out."

For a moment, we sit in silence. Maybe he's thinking of the what-ifs, too.

In a quiet voice Dax asks again, "Could Tyler be mine?"

"I got pregnant on the Fourth of July. He was due mid-May, but they took him a month early; my amniotic fluid was low. I don't see how he could be yours. Justin's an accountant. You think he'd do the math. Tyler was born at thirty-six weeks. If we account for the six-week gap from our last get-together to July Fourth and say he was born full term, then that would have made him forty-two weeks."

"Is that not possible then? Does that not happen?"

When looking at the timeline that way, well...there's a possibility.

"But I had a period between when we were last together and when I was with Justin." Even saying that out loud sounds weak.

"So, you think it might be possible." Dax is leaning forward, nearly vibrating off the couch.

"Maybe." What if Dax is Tyler's dad? I cover my mouth in horror. "I never even considered you. I had a period. There was no reason to think..." I struggle to wrap my brain around the possibility.

If this is true, what comes next?

CHAPTER 21

MONDAY NIGHT

TYLER'S EXHAUSTED BY THE TIME HE AND DOUG COME HOME. He falls asleep on the couch, and I carry him to bed without waking him. By the time I have him tucked in, Josie and Jayne have arrived and are in the kitchen with Dax.

Josie's looking at the papers Justin gave me. She doesn't even glance up when I enter the room. "Did you do the test?"

"Yes," I say and sit in the chair next to her. Dax offers me a hard cider, and I accept. My nerves are shot.

We let Josie read in silence.

"Wow," she says. "He wants you to pay him back within ninety days once the test determines he's not Tyler's dad."

My anger stirs, I say, "How would I be able to do that?"

"He says if you can't do that, he'll take the twelve thousand you have in your account as the down payment and follow that with monthly payments for one year."

Dax slides off the counter he's been sitting on. "How does he know you have twelve grand in your account?" Apparently, his anger is stirring, too.

I shrug. "We didn't have a joint account, and I switched

banks when we divorced. But it's almost on-the-nose exactly how much I have saved. That's the money I was going to use to offset my loss of income when I did my student teaching."

Jayne says, "It's odd he knows how much you have."

Josie taps my phone. "Any chance you have spyware on here or your computer?"

Dax says, "Could he guess your password?"

All these questions are too much. Spyware? I hand Josie my phone, then stand to get my laptop. After retrieving it, I sit, plug in my password, and wait for the page to load. I scan my bank's website and find a tracker that logs when I signed in. Sure enough, there are more sign-ins to my account than the ones I've done.

I swivel the screen to Dax. "He's been logging in. Or someone has."

Josie rolls her eyes. "Don't be nice. It's okay to accuse him. How do you think he got your password?"

"He was carrying your laptop when he found me in the living room the other day."

I think it over, wondering. When we divorced, I made sure to put as large a separation between us possible. Tyler was the only link. And though I tried to keep our lives separate, I also went for an amicable relationship. Clearly that message was lost on Justin.

"I keep a book in my dresser drawer where I log all important info. Like passwords," I say.

Dax says, "That should be in a safe."

I say, "Duh, and when I have a safe, I'll put it in there."

He holds up his hands in apology.

Jayne pats Dax on the shoulder. "Now we know he's been coming in and breaking things, tapping into your accounts, and who knows what else. Bloody wanker. Do we know why?"

I shake my head and type Justin's name in a search engine. "Right after our divorce, Justin changed firms and didn't pay child support for a quarter because he claimed he was unemployed."

Josie snaps her fingers, recognition on her face. "I remember that. We tried to prove he was out of work for only two weeks."

"Cost me a grand, remember?"

She nods. "He gives, and he takes it back."

I point to the screen where I've pulled up his firm's website. "He's now an associate partner with that firm. That's why he has the new car, clothes, and hairstyle. He's damn well making enough money to pay child support."

Jayne asks, "Could a woman be involved?"

Josie takes my computer and does some searching. She's got mad skills. "Nothing remarkable is popping up."

Dax clears his throat. "Do you think maybe my presence set him off? I know that sounds vain, and I'm not trying to make this about me, but he accused Heather of harboring feelings for me while they were married."

I study Dax, then glance at each of my friends. "Dax did come up in the conversation a lot. Justin called him a cash cow."

Josie taps a finger on the table in thought. Then says, "I've seen weirder situations, but here's my take." She looks at me. "You asked for the divorce, remember? He wasn't happy at all. At the deposition, he kept saying he didn't understand why you were leaving him. By his account, he was a stand-up dad and husband. He gave you a house, a child, you stayed home, had spending money, and were allowed to see your friends."

Jayne says, "I remember you telling us about that. You didn't like how he said 'allowed.' Said he sounded possessive."

I recalled the conversation. It worried me at the time. "Josie, you also said to watch out for him to possibly stalk me. But he never did."

She raises her brows. "Didn't he? What's he been doing all this time? Breaking things, thinking you'll call him for help, logging into your bank account? But, thankfully, you're incredibly stubborn and determined to do everything on your own. And you don't call him."

Jayne mumbles, "Or anyone really."

Josie points to Jayne as if what Jayne's said adds to her point. "You don't call him, so he escalates. He monitors your money. Tries to keep you from achieving your dreams by forcing you to use money on lawyers instead of school."

She has a point. And it sends goosebumps up and down my arms. I attempt to rub them away, as if it will solve all the problems.

Josie says, "You need an alarm."

Dax growls. "We're having an alarm installed tomorrow. And whatever else it takes to make this place safe."

"I can't afford that," I tell him.

"I can, and I won't take no—" His phone rings, interrupting my rebuttal and the likely ensuing argument. He glances at the screen, then looks surprised.

"I have to take this." He quickly hops into the living room. The sliding door opening tells me he's taking the call outside.

"He moves fast for a guy with a brace," Josie says.

Jayne sits next to me. "Let him do this for you, Heather. Because if he doesn't put one in, Stacy and Brinn will."

I nod. She's right. Safety over pride.

Jayne continues, keeping her voice low, "Is it possible Tyler is his?"

I tell them about having my period and the six weeks between Dax and Justin.

Josie bites her lip, her tell that she's doing the math. "Unlikely, but possible."

I lean back in my chair and sigh. "Excuse me while I have a pity party." I blink back tears.

"Darling," Jayne says. "You're entitled to a massive temper tantrum if you want." She takes my hand.

"My life is a shit show. My ex wants to disown his kid, maybe his kid, and he's been stalking me. My one-night stand, old college flame, has turned into weeks, and I'm getting used to him being around. But if this doesn't make him run the other way, maybe whoever is calling will make a good enough offer to keep him around." The words get caught in my throat, pushed back by my tears.

Josie leaps from her chair and wraps me in a hug. "I will fry Justin, simply on principle, because he deserves it. Once we get the test results back, we'll get *you* a new BMW to drive."

I know her words are an attempt to make me laugh, but I can't. Because I don't care that Justin wants out of our lives. I'm sad for Tyler. I'm angry for Tyler. He deserves better. And maybe he'll get that with Dax. If Dax is his father. But where does that leave us? I married Justin out of the misguided belief it was what I was supposed to do. I won't repeat that mistake.

Dax being the stand-up guy he is, it's a safe assumption he'll offer the works.

I think about how little I know about him. How we've been living a bit in the past. Only the present has caught up with us now.

If I had one wish, it would be to see into the future.

CHAPTER 22

LATE MONDAY NIGHT

AFTER MY FRIENDS LEAVE, I SIT ON MY BED CHANGING passwords to everything possible. For all I know, Justin was even using my Netflix.

Dax lays stretched out next to me, trying to scratch beneath his cast with a pencil he found on my nightstand. We've been mindful to not make staying in my room a habit, careful of the message we're sending to Tyler. When Tyler wakes up, Dax is always asleep on the couch.

"Stupid plastic hangers," he says. "Are wire ones really so bad?" He cuts his eyes to me and frowns. Two mangled plastic hangers are on the floor, having failed at being useful in the task.

I chuckle. His phone sits on the nightstand, and I glance at it, wondering what secrets it holds.

I finish changing my passwords and close the laptop.

"Well, that's sufficiently creepy, knowing my privacy has been invaded on all levels."

Dax snorts in agreement. "Maybe you can start saving some money now that he's not coming around breaking everything. And the company will be here tomorrow to set up the alarm system. I'll take care of all that and show you how to use it when you get home from work."

"If they come after two, I think I can leave early to be here." Even though doing so would cause me money loss in my paycheck, it would be worth it.

"Nah, I'll show you everything."

He continues to maneuver the pencil around in his cast.

"We should talk," I say, even though I don't want to. I'm exhausted, and today's cost has been heavy emotionally. But what little sleep I might get won't happen if I don't address the elephant in the room.

I slide my laptop onto my nightstand and sit cross-legged facing Dax.

He says, "Would it be better if we slept on everything?"

Having a serious conversation is kinda hard when the bare-chested man in your bed works manically at scratching his leg with a pencil, moaning occasionally when it hits the spot. And as much as I'd love to sleep on all this or, heck, not ever talk about it, that's not an option.

"I can't. There's too much not being said, and I can't pretend it'll wait."

"Okay," he says and readjusts so he's sitting more upright on the bed. He's still messing with the pencil.

"When we hooked up, it was for one night."

He nods, and a grin plays at the corner of his mouth. "But I had this great idea about a second night and talked you into it."

Taking a more light-hearted route would be easier, but I fear wouldn't be clearer. "My point is, this"—I gesture to him then myself—"was supposed to be causal. A few nights, and then we go our separate ways"

He looks up as if thinking, "I don't remember that part. I thought we said we'd take it one night at a time."

"Yeah, and now how many nights later you're looking at the possibility of becoming an overnight dad and changing the whole trajectory of your life."

He shakes his head. "The paternity outcome won't change the trajectory of my life."

"If you're Tyler's dad, I want you to know that I don't expect anything."

He looks at me puzzled. "You should expect something. Care to define what it is you aren't expecting?"

Jeez, this is more awkward than I thought. I struggle to find the words. How do I tell the man that I don't expect him to keep sleeping with me in the event that he's gonna be paying me child support?

Like a fish, my mouth flaps open, but no sounds come out. Finally, I say, "We can sleep on it."

He leaves the pencil sticking out of his cast, then takes my hand. "Heather, I thought we both were trying to be more open. Have better communication. Just say it. Whatever it is."

I press my lips together, and I say the words over and over in my head. Then I close my eyes and blurt out, "You don't have to marry me if Tyler's yours."

I open one eye and peek at Dax. He's smiling at me.

He says, "I know that. This isn't the fifties. First, we get the results, and we go from there. Either way, lots of paths to take." He shrugs one shoulder then resumes his pencil scratching.

I'm oddly disappointed. Did I want him to say we'd run off and get married and live happily ever after? Because the practical side of me says that's ridiculous. The logistics alone, where I want to work and where I live and Dax's uncharted path, likely won't align. Who knows where he'll end up?

But this isn't about being practical. This is about so much more than that. The thought of not having to go at this life alone has ginormous appeal. Having Dax to share the day-to-day and shoulder some of the burdens would be like winning the lottery. Only better.

Over the small number of days he's been here, I've fantasized about having him around longer. About him fixing things that break and protecting me from all the bad things life will doubtless throw at me.

How selfish does that sound?

I've gone and done exactly what I said I didn't want to do. Everything I fought against has happened. I've come to depend on Dax. I want to be rescued by Dax.

Yeah, I'm exhausted and scared after finding out what Justin's been doing. I don't feel safe or protected. Maybe that's why I no longer want to go at this alone. When I'm with Dax, he makes me feel both safe and protected.

I glance at Dax, who is looking down his leg into his cast, one eye open as he maneuvers the pencil like NASA did with the Mars Rover, with fierce intention and purpose.

Dear Lord. What am I doing? Eventually, Dax will not be staying here. He'll get a boot for his leg, and the freedom that comes with that. And even if we find out he's Tyler's father and he lives right next door, he won't be *here* and I'll feel his absence on a grand scale.

Damn. Being a single mom takes a whole lot of energy and willpower.

I glance up at the ceiling in an effort to fight back tears. Scared that I'll not have the strength I've used in the past to get me through. Afraid that having Dax's help has spoiled me, only to make everything else from here on harder.

"What else did you want to talk about?" Dax asks, eyes on his cast.

I have to get out of here. I need to think this out without him nearby. His stupid beefcake-man sexiness is too distracting. Makes logical thought impossible.

I leap from the bed, feeling the familiar heat flush across my chest. I'll be red from chest to cheeks in seconds. And how would I explain that to Dax?

Do I admit my fears to him? That I'm afraid I might be using him to carry my heavy load? Do I confess I want Tyler to be his so he'll stay forever? Or maybe I get angry and say having him in my life makes me a more dependent person and that scares me? Thinking these things is hard enough. Saying them will be impossible.

I grab my robe and hold it to my chest. "Yeah, I'm good. I think I'll take a shower."

He glances at me. "Really? Right now? It's"—he glances at the clock—"midnight."

I nod vigorously. "Yep. I feel very out of sync about all this, and I think if I take a shower, it'll make me feel better."

He stops his quest to scratch the nonstop itch and studies me. "Are you okay?"

I keep nodding like a bobblehead, not looking at him, but at my escape route.

"Heather?"

"Yep, I'm good." Eyes on the hallway, I rush to the door, only to catch my hip on the corner of my bed's wood footboard, throwing me slightly to the side so that I bounce into the wall.

I glance over my shoulder and grimace. I have his full

attention. I say, "I'm good. Real good. So good. Sooo gooood." I stumble toward the bedroom door.

"Yeah, I can see you're good." The skepticism in his voice indicates he doesn't believe me.

I spin, robe clutched to my chest, and face him as I backpedal out the door. "So, so good. Fine." And stupid, because I can't think of anything else to say. I close the door behind me and nearly collapse against the wall. But I know Dax. He'll follow me. I waste no time escaping into the bathroom where I lock the door behind me. Instead of a shower, I draw a bath and sink into the warm water.

I have no idea where to go from here.

CHAPTER 23

TUESDAY

THE NEXT MORNING DAX AND I ACT LIKE EVERYTHING IS normal. Well, for him maybe it sorta is. He didn't have any life-altering realizations late last night.

As I hustle Tyler out the door for school, Dax is on my deck Face-Timing a man who I think is his agent. But I can't hear anything of what they're saying. Sometimes, a girl's gotta eavesdrop, or at least try. Even if she does fail.

After I drop Tyler at school, my imagination about what Dax and his agent are discussing goes into overdrive, so I pull into an empty parking lot and do some internet searching.

Bleacher Report has a breaking story about Dax's dad. He's leaving the Tampa head coach position to be the General Manager of a New York team. The report talks about how they expect Coach Griffin will clean house and start over with new coaching staff as this NY team's record for the last two years was six and ten. A losing record.

The sports reporter then speculates who will fill the

suddenly vacated positions, and Dax's name is at the top of the list.

Was that what his phone call last night was about? His dad calling him to offer him a job? And now he's talking to his agent who will work out the specifics of the contract?

The position would make Dax's career. Should he want a career in coaching, that is. Only, I don't actually know what Dax wants. I thought maybe he didn't know either since he told me how he's felt aimless up until now.

Would I move to New York if he asked? Never mind that I'm not sure he would ask.

I shake my head. No. Tyler's doctors are amazing, and we're only at the beginning of the very long process of getting him stabilized. And we've been successful so far. I would never want to disrupt that. How long will the process last? No one knows. Everything depends on the information we gather through all the testing. No, leaving the general area is not an option for me.

And just like that, all my fears resurface again. Knowing I predicted this possibility is no comfort. It's inevitable that Dax will be moving on simply because there are no jobs for him in Daytona Beach. Not unless he wants to be a high school coach or something. That might work in the short term, but eventually he'd want more. He won't be staying in the area, and I'd better get used to that right now.

Even if he is Tyler's dad, the man has to make money. The man has to have a fulfilling career. I would never begrudge him that.

It's like college all over again. I take several deep breaths and get control of my racing thoughts. I will not handle this like college. I'll see how this plays out.

I nod as if doing so sets my determination in stone, when

all I really want to do is run and protect my heart and my child.

After a brief pep talk, I head to work, driving through the post office at the last minute because I almost forgot to drop off the paternity kit.

Moments later, I get an email saying the kit has been submitted and will ship to the laboratory today. I forward it to Justin and his lawyer just in case they want to say I didn't submit it within the given timeframe.

Now we wait.

And I'm the champ at waiting. I've put off luxuries and vacations and so much more as I work to finish school. As I wait for child support checks. I got this.

Inside the boutique, I'm in the back sorting the new inventory and making a list of what needs to be done today when Jayne enters.

"Hello, darling. I brought scones and tea and fortune cookies." Dressed in a navy-blue leather shift dress with a V-neck, bright sunflower-yellow three-inch heels, her hair pulled into a French twist, Jayne looks the part of a successful businesswoman. A woman whose life isn't a mess.

She puts her containers on the table next to me. Then hands me a fortune cookie. "Open it. Mine this morning was spectacular. It said, 'You will find your love today.' Which I did. Because after I got Cordie on the bus, Stacy and I sexed each other up in the kitchen. That man may approach sex like a mathematical equation that needs to be solved, but damn if I don't enjoy it every time. Who knew having an orgasm among the carbs would be so glorious. Which is why I'm late, sorry." She clasps her hands and points to my cookie, eager for me to open it.

Jayne lives her life by fortune cookies. She has a jar of

saved fortunes she's collected over the years. On bad days, she'll go to the jar and take one out, looking for inspiration or a pick-me-up. Many of her saved fortunes say, *Go buy shoes.*

"Okay," I tease. "I'll open it, but don't expect any hanky panky between us in the back room." But even as I say it, there's not a lot of merriment in my voice.

Jayne laughs, but it doesn't last long. She narrows her eyes. "You all right?"

I nod and focus on opening the wrapper. "I'm good." I stop there, not wanting to sound like the loon I did last night.

I gently slide the fortune from between the folded cookie halves. Then I unfold the paper. I read, "Don't determine the end of the story by the middle."

Jayne quirks her head to the side. "I suppose that's decent."

My response is to burst into tears. So much for being in control.

"I'm sorry," I say, flapping my hands by my eyes, as if fanning them will make my tears dry up. "I don't know why I'm crying."

Jayne leans back against the worktable we use to unpack inventory, her hands on either side. "Well, first I'd say you've had a crazy few weeks. The latest with Justin is just rotten icing on a moldy cake."

I nod and wipe my nose on tissue paper that came in a box with Italian leather boots. "Never mind that he's been stalking me. I still can't wrap my head around that."

Jayne hands me a tissue. "And then there's Dax."

I spill my guts. Everything. The report I saw online. How I know he'll leave, and I don't want him to go.

"But that's wonderful," she says.

I shake my head. "It's not wonderful to use a person, because that's what I'm doing. I'm using him to make my life better. To rescue me. How many times have I said I don't need a knight in shining armor?" I don't wait for an answer. "Well, I guess I lied because this guy's been around my house fixing stuff for two weeks, and I want to keep him. I want to enslave him."

Her brows go up. "That's a wee bit dramatic, don't you think? Enslave? Really?"

I plop into the chair beside the table. "Yes, it's totally dramatic, but I have all these feelings. They're so intense. It's like I'm...." I struggle to find the best way to describe the turmoil inside me.

Jayne says, "Would you say you feel enslaved by your feelings?"

I glance up in time to see the twitches on her lips, as she struggles to restrain her smile.

"Yes," I say. "I'm enslaved. Am I going to live that down?"

Jayne shakes her head. "Certainly not. And when I tell the others..."

I bury my head in my hands and groan.

Jayne says, "You know, having all these feelings is normal. You're working it out. That's all."

"You're right, but I feel like a douchebag. Like I've been using him."

Jayne pulls up a chair, and before she sits, she grabs the box of scones. Once in her seat, she flips it open and offers me one.

I take it and break off the pointy end.

Jayne says, "Do you think the issue is that you are using

him, or maybe there's something more?" She takes a scone and bites off the end.

I play with mine. "Like what?"

She studies me a second before she says, "Maybe you have stronger feelings than—"

"No, it's too soon. We barely know each other."

Jayne gives me a puzzled look. "But you actually do know him. It's not like you just met."

"We're different people now," I argue.

She drops her scone onto the table. "All I'm saying is, maybe you have a crush on Dax? Maybe that's why you envision him taking care of you. Maybe you're tired of going it alone. All of which is normal."

I do one of those ragged breaths people take after they've been crying as I work to calm down. "Yeah, both Tyler and I have a crush on Dax. Different crushes, of course."

"Of course." She nods. "It's been a while since you've been in this place—the crush zone." She smiles at me. "Maybe give yourself a little grace to fumble your way through it." She points to the fortune cookie. "And maybe, just maybe, you shouldn't make any more assumptions about what needs to happen until you have to make a decision about what to do. Because right now, do you have to make any decision?"

She has a point. I shake my head. "You don't think I'm being unfair to him?"

Jayne smooths her dress. "That's a different question. And one I don't think you'd like to hear the answer to."

CHAPTER 24

TUESDAY NIGHT

By the time I get home, I've composed myself and had enough self-talks that I'm thoroughly confused about how I feel.

What I do know is when I see Dax, I experience happiness. What I'm confused about is the why. Am I happy because he's there to protect and save me, or for reasons more genuine? Like I'm happy to see my friend.

Dax is at the kitchen table working on his laptop. Tyler is next to him working on his homework.

"What's going on here?" I set the groceries for tacos on the kitchen counter.

"The men are working," Dax says with a wink.

Tyler smiles up at me. "We're using our big brains. I'm using mine to do math, and Dax is using his to show his football smarts."

The way he says it, I know he's quoting Dax.

I glance at Dax. "Trivia contest or something?"

He shakes his head. "Proving I'm worthy."

What a cryptic answer. Or I'm reading into everything. Could be both.

"Tacos?" I say.

Tyler makes a face, and not a good one.

"What? You like tacos," I say.

Tyler gives a nonchalant shrug. "I'm over tacos. Can we get takeout or have steak or something?"

I feign disbelief. "You're over tacos? No one gets over tacos. Tacos span time." I look at Dax. "I blame you. You bring your fancy grilling technique and online food ordering skills to the house, and now my kid's a food critic. He's over tacos."

Dax laughs. "What if we call them street tacos. Put them on those smaller shells. Does that appeal to you?" he asks Tyler.

Tyler gives a small nod, his nose raised in the air ever so slightly. "I'll try it."

"I don't have small shells," I say.

Dax says, "Do you have regular tortillas?"

I nod.

"We'll just cut smaller ones from those."

Tyler gives a thumbs-up then taps his head. "Big brains."

"Yep," I say. My first thought is cutting smaller ones from the large ones is a waste. And something I would never ever do because money doesn't grow on trees. But Dax is here, so we break the rules. And even though his idea is wasteful, it's also frivolous and fun, and I love those things. I'd forgotten what frivolous feels like.

I turn back to the groceries, not wanting Dax to see my face, worried the pleasure of my addiction to his disruption of our lives will show.

A chair behind me scrapes against the floor and, when I turn, Dax is lifting himself up.

"Let me show you this alarm," he says.

I toss the few groceries in the fridge and follow Dax into the hallway, where the wall is devoid of any alarm system. Only his crutches lean against the wall.

I look around confused. "Where is it?"

"Right here," he says and backs me up against the wall. With his hands on my hips, he dips his head to brush a kiss across my mouth. Three times. I melt into him.

I mumble against his lips. "What are you doing?"

"Saying hello." When he presses his pelvis to mine, I nearly lose my mind with desire. I forget about everything that bogged my mind down today and let myself get lost in pleasure.

As he braces himself with one hand against the wall, Dax moves the other hand up my shirt, and his lips are on my collar bone kissing a path toward my breast. I run a hand up his leg and under his athletic shorts and grasp him, stroking softly once. He sucks in a breath. My move fans the flames. He's hard. I'm wet. His desire for me as strong as mine for him. And our need to quench this thirst carries both of us away. Our tempo increases. Dax's hand slides from under my shirt to up my skirt where he toys with the seam of my panties. I tremble. He groans. Tyler's chair scrapes across the floor in the kitchen.

The sound brings me to my senses, and I push Dax away. He hobbles back, trying to balance on one leg, his hand over his man parts covering his erection.

"Jeez, that got out of hand fast," he says with a grin, leaning against the wall for support.

I sink to the floor because my legs are weak and my hands are shaking and I still want him.

Tyler comes into the room. "Can I start cutting the thingies?"

"Yes," Dax says.

"No," I say.

Dax gives me the eye and glances down to his hands. His way of saying he needs Tyler to leave the room right away.

"Okay," I say to them both but look at Tyler. "You can cut them, but first you need to set everything up. Get out a cutting board and the tortillas. I'll be there in a minute."

Tyler smiles and zips off back to the kitchen.

Dax blows out a breath and gestures for me to follow him into the living room, then grabs his crutches. "Grab your phone," he calls over his shoulder.

In the living room, he's plopped on the couch. I sit on the coffee table and face him, afraid to be next to him or I might jump his bones. My body is not ready to stop what we started.

He takes my phone and adds an app. Once it's loaded, he shows me where all the cameras are and how to check each one remotely. He shows me how to activate or deactivate the alarm, all from my phone. "You can do it from the website on your computer, too."

I smile. "Cool. Did it take long to install this?"

Dax shakes his head. "No, and I got a few extra cameras thrown in because the technician is a fan. You'll never have to worry about someone coming in here again without you knowing. You having this gives me peace of mind." He shows me his phone. "I'm going to delete the app from my phone. Only you should have it. And you should change your pass-word. I only had it to show you."

The gesture is sweet. He's telling me he's not going to invade my privacy the way Justin did. But I can't help but read more into it. That he's leaving. That he won't have this connection with us. Ugh, I don't know. Maybe I'm being stupid. Yet, it's how I feel.

My phone pings, and I check my email. "Look." I show him the email. "The lab got the package, and the result will be available in twenty-four hours."

"Wow, that was fast."

I nod. "Yeah, I guess Justin paid for the fastest delivery possible. He really wants to be done with us."

"He's an idiot." Dax squeezes my knee.

Tyler yells from the kitchen, "Okay, I'm ready."

Dax and I grin at each other. I stand as Dax's phone rings. He glances at the screen, and a slight smile plays on his lips. He takes his earbuds from his pocket and places them in his ears. As he's doing so, he says, "Hand me a crutch, will ya? I'm going to take this outside." Then he answers the call. I hand him a crutch and watch him hobble out to the patio. Not looking back once.

In the kitchen, I place my phone on the table next to Dax's computer and go help Tyler.

"Okay," I say. "We need something round." I take a plastic cup from the cabinet. "We can use this. Watch." I flip the cup upside down and go around it with a butter knife. "If the knife doesn't cut all the way, you hand it to me and I'll finish the job." Because handing him a butter knife is scary enough, I won't go with anything sharper.

Standing on a kitchen step-stool so he can reach easier, Tyler gets right to work, a grin on his face. "This is cool."

I'm glad simple pleasures work for him.

My phone chimes a message, and I walk to the table to

check it. Only it's not my phone but Dax's computer. I don't mean to read it, even though I do have snooping tendencies. But there's the message, hanging out in the corner of the computer screen.

It's from his dad and it reads: *Excited to have you as part of the team. I can have our realtor look for a place for you while she looks for us. Yes?*

And it's like college all over again. Dax is leaving.

CHAPTER 25

WEDNESDAY

HOW I MADE IT THROUGH LAST NIGHT WILL REMAIN A MYSTERY. Maybe it was because Dax was on his phone or computer most of the night doing whatever. The shit-eating grin on his face clarified that he was happy with whatever it was.

I had some assignments to finish. After I got Tyler to bed, I stared at my notes for far too long, then finally got lost in my studies. When I shut it down at midnight, Dax was asleep on the couch.

I set the alarm and went to bed, feeling miles away from him.

Funny how a few weeks ago I challenged the universe to bring it, and here it all was. And the universe brought its A-game.

I rise before my alarm and dress in silence as I trudge through my heavy thoughts.

I'm in the kitchen making coffee when my phone pings with an incoming email. Out of habit, I glance to see if it's anything important.

It's from the laboratory doing the paternity test. Holy

crap, that was fast. I set my mug on the counter and stare at the email, leaving it unopened.

Dax hops into the kitchen. "Hey, why didn't you wake me when you went to bed? I woke up cuddling Tyler's stuffed animal, thinking it was you." He drops a kiss on my forehead.

I glance between him and the phone.

He pours coffee into the mug I abandoned. "What? Something wrong?"

"The paternity results are in."

"No shit? What's it say?" He grabs at my phone, but I hold it out of reach. "Come on, let's see it."

"Dax, I feel like we should say things. I..."

But I don't know what. It's so much, all these feelings.

He brushes a hand down my cheek. "Babe, what are you afraid of?"

"You leaving," I say. The truth tumbles out. Not because he might be the father of my kid. But because the results of this test feel like something big that could make or break everything.

Because somewhere between midnight and this morning, it dawned on me what Jayne meant. I love Dax. The thought of him not coming around anymore makes my heart race with anxiety and loneliness. All along, I've been preparing for him to leave because I can't imagine why he'd want to stay. What can I offer him? A ready-made family? He may not want that. Yes, the sex is out of this world. But a couple can't exist on sex alone.

But I want him to do chores around my house because I want to share my house with him. Having him here this short time has been everything I hoped my marriage could have been and everything I imagine a healthy relationship should be. I don't want to let that go.

Acknowledging that I can't control what happens now, and the fear that comes with that, causes a chain reaction of all my emotions, colliding and pouring out of me.

This is about so much more than having someone to share the workload with. This is about love. I am in love with Dax. Heck, I probably have always been in love with him, having never really moved on. Because moving on from something that feels so right and natural feels so wrong and unnatural.

Dear Lord, Justin was right. To a degree, Dax always stood between us. Not purposeful on my part, but as I struggled to make a difficult marriage work, I'm sure the realization that I walked away from something I wanted more was always there subconsciously.

And here we are again.

Tears stream down my face. "I know you're taking that job in New York, and I'm happy you found something you want, but I don't want you to go. And if you're Tyler's dad, does that mean I'll have to send him to you there? How will that work? Because you can already tell that Tyler being out of my sight is not good for me. I don't handle that well."

He pulls me into his arms. "Heather, why didn't you talk this out with me? I thought we were trying to not repeat college."

I rest my forehead on his shoulder and give in to my tears.

"Babe, what makes you think I'm taking the job in New York? I told you I didn't want to work for my dad."

"I saw his text to you last night. While you were on the phone."

Dax groans. "My dad can't take no for an answer. Which I've said to him at least one hundred times daily. That text didn't say I took the job. It said he wanted me on the team. His way of telling me how disappointed he'll be if I don't take the job."

I wipe my face on his T-shirt, not caring that I left a mascara smudge. I pull back to look up at him. "You aren't going to New York?"

He shakes his head. "I wanted to tell you this later. I have a whole plan in motion, but I can see that making you wait might not have been the best move."

My eyes narrow. "What are you talking about?"

"I took the assistant coach job for the university in Orlando. It's the closest I could get to Daytona."

"When did this happen?" My brain is slowly processing what he's just said.

"Well, that day I was here with you and Tyler, the night after you sexed me up in the minivan? I asked my agent if there was anything nearby that might work for me. He called and said the university might be interested, but I had to meet with them that day since the head coach was headed out of town the following day."

"That's why you rushed out of here?"

"Yep." He wipes moisture from my cheek.

"I thought we weren't going to keep stuff like this from each other?"

He smiles. "I know, and I felt terrible, but I really wanted it to work out, and I was afraid to bring it up. And what if I didn't get the job? All of it felt like a lot to load on you when you weren't even sure you wanted me to come back even one more day. Remember?"

I nod. "So, you're moving to Orlando?" I'm still wrapped in his arms.

"I wasn't joking when I said I'd been aimless until I ran into you. Throwing the football out here with Tyler helped me decide on my next course."

My phone, which has been pressed into my hand and his waist, buzzed. I glanced at the screen. Josie.

"She wants to go over the results I'm sure." I show him the screen.

He meets my gaze. "Can we see them together first?"

"If you want. Are you sure?"

He smiles. "I know you think a lot would change for me, but I disagree."

"Everything would change for you," I say, incredulous.

He puts up a finger. "Wait right here." He hops backward, mumbling. "Why did I bother to make a plan? Nothing is going like I planned." He hobbles out of the room.

I sip coffee while I wait, desperate to take a peek. I text Josie that we're going to look at the results now and will call her ASAP.

Dax hops back in and comes to a stop before me. He smiles then drops to one knee, kicking out his broken leg to one side. "Damn, this is uncomfortable."

"What are you doing?" I say.

He takes my hand in his. "Heather Lowell Michaels. Will you marry me? I don't care what that paternity test says. I want Tyler and I want you, not in that order, equally. I want this." He gestures to the house. "I want to come home to you every night. I want to make street taco shells from big tortillas. I want to play catch with Tyler and go to the doctors with you. I want to take care of him and do everything in my power to make him healthy. I want to give him siblings. And I want…"

I clap my hand over his mouth. "Stop." I shake my head. "I can't take it. I can't believe this is happening. I love you, and I was afraid you might not feel the same about me, and all *this* might be the last thing you would ever want."

"Help me up," he says. My hand is still in his, and he presses something into my palm.

I open my hand to find a diamond ring.

Dax says, "I'm going to take your declaration of love as a yes."

"Yes," I say. Then pause. "Oh, you have to ask Tyler. That's the right thing to do."

He dismisses me with a wave of his hand. "Already did that last night."

"Wait, you and Tyler discussed this, and he kept it a secret?"

"Yep. Discussed it over ice cream before you came home. Ice cream before dinner. He kept that secret, too."

I laugh and look at the ring. Amazed at how today has unfolded. "Marry you," I say, as if the impossible has happened. I look at Dax, tears in my eyes. "I don't think I've ever wanted to be with anyone else, ever."

He sweeps me up into a hug and nuzzles my neck. I hold him close. "Me neither. No one ever felt right like you do. I have always loved you."

"And I have always loed you."

My phone chimes again.

Dax says, "We should look. But now do you see why I kept saying whatever the results are, they won't change my trajectory? Because where you and Tyler are is where I want to be."

I pull back and against him as I engage my phone and open my email app. "Ready?"

He nods.

I click on the email and scan the details.

"Well, hell," Dax says, disappointed.

"Justin is Tyler's dad."

CHAPTER 26

WEDNESDAY MORNING

DAX TAKES THE PHONE AND SETS IT ON THE COUNTER. HE turns me to face him. "I have a solution for that if you're up for hearing my next crazy idea."

"Are you saying marrying me is crazy?" I hold out the ring to him, teasing that he could take it back. He takes it from me and slips it on my finger. It fits perfectly. I look at him surprised. Everything about the ring is...well, perfect. Even the simple design with the round stone.

"I had your mom's help. She sent a collection of bride magazines that I hid in the closet. And I used one of the rings in your jewelry box to find your size," he says, knowing my question without me having to ask it. "And no, not crazy in a bad way. Crazy in all the best ways." With his hands on my hips, he pulls me to him. His hands go to my backside and cup my butt.

"Is this your solution? Sex in the kitchen?" Because I'm down for it.

"Nope, I want to adopt Tyler. I want to make Justin a deal that makes him walk away for good. Maybe that's not the right thing to want, a dad to leave his kid, but he doesn't deserve Tyler."

I take his face between my hands and search his face. "Dax, are you serious?"

"Yeah, I want that kid to be mine. I desperately wanted this test to prove it, too."

The kid in question shuffles into the kitchen and stops short when he sees us. "What's going on? Why are you crying, momma?"

I point to my face. "These are happy tears, baby."

Dax pulls out a kitchen chair and sits. He gestures to Tyler for him come. "I got bad news, buddy. Remember that plan we had to give your mom the ring?"

Tyler's eyes go wide. "It was a secret."

"Yeah, I know, but I had to blow the secret. I'm sorry."

Tyler looks between Dax and me. "But does that mean we're all going to live together forever? Or not?"

I kneel beside Tyler. "Are you okay with us living together forever? If we keep Dax?"

Tyler's nods are emphatic.

"I want to stay with Dax forever, too," I say.

Tyler leans into me and says in a soft voice, "I wish he was my dad."

I wrap him in my arms and glance at Dax. "He will be baby. He doesn't have to have the same last name to be your dad." Explaining it to a child is beyond complicated. I don't mention Dax's suggestion of adoption because there's no telling how Justin will react. But I want Tyler to know that a person doesn't have to be biologically related to be a father.

I look at Dax again, "Let's do it," I say. "I'll give him all my savings if he wants." It's bold and scary to ask a man to give up paternity rights to his child. But Justin never wanted to be

Tyler's dad anyway. I only hope one day Tyler will understand.

Dax reaches for his phone. "Are you sure?"

I nod.

Tyler says, "Can I have frozen waffles?"

"Yes, but you have to heat them up," I say as my son pulls away and goes to the fridge.

"Do I have to go to school today?"

I roll my eyes. "Of course, you do."

Dax reaches for his phone and makes a call. "Hi, this is Dax Griffin calling for Mr. Taylor. I was in his office two days ago asking about adoption. Please tell him to start the paperwork. Thank you." He disconnects and puts the phone down. "Voicemail. I forgot it's stupid early."

I laugh. "You already talked to a lawyer?"

He nods. "Yeah, I might have wanted a miracle, but I wasn't leaving it all to chance."

"Hand me my phone," I say. Dax passes it over. I call Josie. I tell her the news and our plans.

Dax takes the phone from me and says, "Josie, spare no expense. Let's end this." Following a brief pause he laughs and says, "Tell that to Heather."

He hands the phone back to me and I say, "What's so funny?"

Josie says, "There won't be any expense from me because it would be my greatest pleasure to make Justin squirm before we cut him loose."

"I just want this to be over," I say and look between Tyler and Dax.

Josie says, "I know. I'm asking you to dig deep one more time and fight. I'm only going to ask for what he owes you to date. We know he doesn't want to give you the money, so I want to have an unbiased financial advisor put the money in an account for Tyler. He can it for college or a car or whatever. That person can manage Justin's payments until he's all caught up. You won't ever have to deal with him. But he needs to be made to do the right thing. Justin's lucky Dax loves Tyler and wants to be a part of his life. He can show his appreciation by doing the right thing."

She makes a good argument. Which is why she's such a good lawyer, I suppose. I look at Dax, silently asking if this is what we should do. He nods.

"Okay," I say. "Go for it."

"Hot damn," she says. "I'll call you as soon as I know more."

And just like that, my life changes.

EPILOGUE
FIVE MONTHS LATER

WE PLANNED AN AFTERNOON WEDDING, A SMALL AFFAIR AT Josie's house. We let the view of the beach from her backyard be our backdrop.

The last few months haven't been easy. Justin tried to get out of paying anything and instead insisted Dax buy Tyler from him. Which only angered me more and steeled my resolve to make him pay at least something.

But the threat of having his wages garnished and his credit ruined were enough to make Justin see reason. He paid up and signed away his legal rights as Tyler's father.

Both Dax and I started our new positions within days of each other. Which made logistics difficult since we both worked in Orlando but wanted Tyler to finish out his school year in Daytona. But once school was done, we sold my house and bought a house in Lake Mary, halfway between Orlando and Daytona. Dax insisted on a gated community, and after having Justin break into my house for the last few years, I didn't put up much resistance.

Only two weeks ago, I completed my internship as a child life specialist and will start my position in another two weeks, after the honeymoon. For Dax, we have a narrow window of freedom before school starts and football season begins.

But now, we're ready for this new chapter. I miss my friends and not seeing Jayne every day, but we still talk all the time. With Paisley leaving for Japan in a month, we're spending as much time together as we can.

I stand on the edge of Josie's yard, my heels sinking softly into her grass. One large step to my right, and I'm on the beach. My dress is the softest of pinks with a modest sweetheart neckline that flows into an A-line skirt and falls to my ankles. It's sleeveless and simple. There's no veil. My bouquet is pink peonies and white hydrangeas. All of this is Jayne's tasteful work coming together.

Dax is dressed in a light gray suit. His leg has healed, and there's no boot but a regular shoe. Tyler is in a matching suit. They both look dapper, Tyler so grown up. He stands in front of me and looks up at Dax with such love it makes me want to weep with relief.

In attendance are my friends and their partners, my parents, and Doug and Kenley, who cradle the two-month-old they have officially adopted. Dax has invited his parents, his sister, who I enjoyed reconnecting with, her children, and one close friend, the quarterback from his former team.

"Do you, Heather Elizabeth, take Daxton Charles to be your lawfully wedded husband?" The preacher is a local man named Sam Oliver who happens to be the same one who baptized Tyler. He's an older gentleman with graying temples, a warm smile, and a knack for storytelling.

"I do," I say as I look into Dax's eyes.

"Do you, Daxton Charles, take Heather Elizabeth to be your lawfully wedded wife?"

"Yes, please," Dax says.

People in the crowd chuckle.

Pastor Oliver looks down at Tyler, "And do you, Tyler Douglas, take Daxton Charles to be your legal father?"

Tyler nods emphatically. "Yep. Yes, sir."

Pastor Oliver says to Dax, "And do you, Daxton, take Tyler Douglas to be your legal son?"

Dax kneels before Tyler and says, "Yes, I'll be there for you every day. Nothing would make me prouder than to be your dad."

Tyler throws himself into Dax's arms.

I have been given more than I ever thought possible. If this gift is mine because of all the hard times when I had to go it alone, then I'd do it all over again. And again, and again.

Dax, having lifted Tyler and holding him at his side, finishes his vows. We slide on the rings and make it official.

Dax says, "I'm gonna set you down, buddy, so I can kiss your mom."

Tyler smiles at me as Dax lowers him to the ground.

Dax pulls me into his arms and says, "If you had one wish?"

But I don't need to wish. I have everything a girl could ever want.

———

Enjoyed this series and wondering where to go next? You can pick your own adventure.

1. If you're looking for more sexy time and like cowboys then check out my Wyoming Matchmaker Series

2. If you liked the friends, the laughs, and enjoy a good mystery then check out my Samantha True Mystery Series.

BOOKS BY KRISTI ROSE

The No Strings Attached Series-

(Romance) The No Strings Series has a chick lit vibe and some are available in audio.

The Girl He Knows

The Girl He Needs

The Girl He Wants

The Girl He Loves

———

Like cowboys?

The Wyoming Matchmaker Series

(Romance) Sweet and sexy romances on the ranch. There's action, adventure, and heartbreaking angst paired with feel good rewards.

The Cowboy Takes A Bride

The Cowboy's Make Believe Bride

The Cowboy's Runaway Bride

———

Samantha True Mysteries

Also in audio

(Mystery) These laugh out loud, action pack books take place in the Pacific Northwest. Join Samantha, an adult with dyslexia who's hid behind photography, on her adventures in her new life as a Private Investigator. A job she inherited when her new husband died unexpectedly and left behind a mess and another wife.

One Hit Wonder

All Bets Are Off

Best Laid Plans

Caught Off Guard

Two Time Loser

Dodged A Bullet

———

The Meryton Brides

(Sweet romance) The Meryton Brides is a complete series (for now) that is a light, pleasant modernization of Jane Austen's Pride and Prejudice with a twist on the characters. These sweet contemporary romance books are full of love, friendship, trust, and family. Darcy and Elizabeth's story spans the series and ends in book 5, but each book provides the happily ever after we seek.

To Have and To Hold (Book 1)

With This Ring (Book 2)

I Do (Book 3)

Promise Me This (Book 4)

Marry Me, Matchmaker (Book 5)

Honeymoon Postponed (Book 6)

Matchmaker's Guidebook - FREE

———

<u>*The Coming Home Series*</u>

(Sweet Romance) A collection of small-town short stories that take place in Lakeland, Florida where Kristi grew up. These sweet romances are bite sized stories of happiness, wit, and laughter and invite you into the lives of 5 women and leave you happy because of the feel, good endings.

Second Chances

Once Again

Reason to Stay

He's the One

Kiss Me Again

or purchased in a bundle for a better discount.

<u>*The Coming Home Series:*</u> A Collection of 5 Second Chance Short Stories (Can be purchased individually).

Love Comes Home

Standalone Mysteries:

Campus Murder Club

Perfect Place (Using pen name Robbie Peale)

JOIN KRISTI'S READER NEWSLETTER

I hope you enjoy this book. I'd love to connect and share more with you. Be a part of my Reader Newsletter and let's get to know each other. There, I'll share all sorts of book information. You're guaranteed to find an escape. You'll also be the first to know about my sales and new releases. You'll have access to giveaways, freebies, and bonus content. Think you might be interested? Give me a try. You can always leave at any time.

If you enjoyed this book I would appreciate if you'd share that with others. I love when my friends pass along a good read. Here's some ways you can help.

Lend it , Recommend it , Review it
XO, Kristi

MEET KRISTI ROSE

Hey! I'm Kristi. I write romances that will tug your heartstrings and laugh out loud mysteries. In all my stories you'll fall in love with the cast of characters, they'll become old, fun friends. **My one hope** is that I create stories that *satisfy any of your book cravings* and offer a get-away from everyday life. When I'm not writing I'm repurposing Happy Planners or drinking a London Fog (hot tea with frothy milk).

I'd love to get to know you better. Join my Read & Relax community and then fire off an email and tell me 3 things about you!

Not ready to join? Email me below or follow me at one of the links below. Thanks for popping by!

You can connect with Kristi at any of the following:
www.kristirose.net
kristi@kristirose.net

www.ingramcontent.com/pod-product-compliance
Lightning Source LLC
Chambersburg PA
CBHW021333190726
48288CB00003B/1082